HOPE'S WISH

GUARDED SOULS

LEXXIE COUPER

Hope's
WISH

Guarded Souls Book Two

LEXXIE COUPER

The characters and events portrayed in this book are fictitious. Any similarity to real persons, living or dead, is purely coincidental and not intended by the author.

Hope's Wish
Copyright © 2019 by Lexxie Couper
Editing by Kelli Collins

DEDICATION

For my eldest daughter, Peanut. Because she noticed I hadn't dedicated this book to anyone and told me I had to dedicate it to her.

HOPE'S WISH

PROLOGUE

"**I** summoned you to save my village, not take my daughter from me!"

Narrowing his eyes at the man raging before him, Barqan shook his head. "*You* killed Rose, Syrin. *I* tried to save her."

The sorcerer snarled, hate and grief boiling in his eyes. The spell—*his* spell, the one he'd cast to end Barqan's existence—was devouring him from the inside out with greedy haste, turning him into an empty shell devoid of life. Killing him. As it had killed Rose.

Barqan couldn't stop that, no matter how desperate the man's unspoken wishes. And they were so desperate, screamed so loudly by his dying soul, Barqan could barely hear anything else.

"She wasn't yours," Syrin yelled. "She was not part of our covenant!"

"I loved her," Barqan stated. In his chest, his heart clenched. Such a fragile thing. How did humans survive the pain of it?

The thick purple smoke churning around him grew

denser, the fraying control he had over his physical state beginning to vanish. Soon his corporeal form would cease to exist. If the sorcerer was still alive when that happened...

He curled his fists. Every molecule of his body thrummed. Soon he would be without solid substance, just ancient intangible power. "And she loved *me*!"

"*Love*?" Contempt twisted the sorcerer's face into a grotesque mask. "A miscreant like you doesn't deserve love. You didn't deserve Rose!" Malevolent rage contorted his face further. "And with my dying breath, I will make sure you never love again!"

The molecules of Barqan's body grew frenetic, wild.

Just as Syrin began his incantation...

Just as Barqan surrendered to the smoke...

1

1 *400 years later*

DAVID BOWIE.

That's all a man needed to decompress.

David Bowie singing "Space Oddity." Add a cold drink to the mix—tonight it was a gin and tonic—and a bowl of pretzels and, in James Hastin's humble opinion, the night could go on forever.

He'd experience more than one night that felt like it would never end during his time in this world. Until Bowie came along, those dragging nights were torturous.

"Why are we at a karaoke bar again?"

Letting a smile curl his lips, James threw the man sitting beside him a sideways look. "I'm feeling generous, Kitt."

Kitt Newton winced, the bar's muted overhead lights flickering in his amber eyes. "I've been told the last time you felt generous, William Shatner was nominated for a Grammy."

James laughed, plucked a pretzel from the bowl in front of him—a bowl that never emptied, regardless of the fact the barkeeper never topped it up—and tossed it into his mouth.

Pretzels fell into the "good" column.

Salted peanuts, though? Those oily little bastards fell into the "bad" column.

"I'm generous far more often than you realize," he said around a mouthful of crunchy, savory deliciousness. "For instance, Taylor Swift."

Kitt shifted on his stool. James didn't need to look at him to see it. The very air around the other man seemed to growl. "You're telling me you're responsible for Taylor Swift's success?"

Grinning, James threw another pretzel into his mouth and chewed.

Kitt frowned, amber eyes catching the light again, and shook his head. "I never know when to believe you, Hastin."

"I never lie, Rover."

Kitt rolled his eyes and snagged a handful of pretzels himself. "Don't call me Rover." He ate the handful in a single bite and scanned the crowd reflected in the bar's mirrored wall. "So who is it?"

Lifting a just-be-patient finger, James closed his eyes and tasted the longing in the air. Flipped through the silent hopes, dreams, aspirations and desires wafting around him.

So many cravings for sex in the place. So many wishes for an accidental brushing of boob on arm, groin on butt.

So many wishes for a quickie in the alley out back, a tangle in the toilet, a blow job in the backseat of an Uber...

Why an Uber?

Didn't matter. If a blow job in the backseat of an Uber was what the wisher wanted, who was he to point out the impact on their user rating?

After the shit-fire madness he'd just been through helping out Guarded Souls' resident fallen angel, he needed a rush. Needed to tap into an emotional high and wallow about for a bit.

Was the high of oral sex in a moving vehicle the kind of rush he was chasing, though?

"Are you still looking?" Kitt grumbled beside him. "Or have you gone to sleep?"

He smiled, opened his eyes and turned on his stool to face the crowd. "There."

Kitt frowned at the writhing mass of people and took a sip of his Scotch. "Who? Which one? Male or female? Give me a clue, dude."

James smiled. "Patience."

She stood—or rather, fidgeted—on the dance floor a few feet from the unused karaoke stage. She was trying to look like she was dancing, but in her heart of hearts, she was wondering what her date (a firefighter who made her feel special and nervous and safe all at once) would do if she climbed onto the stage and requested the karaoke MC tee up Bon Jovi's "Livin' on a Prayer"?

Let's see, shall we?

James brushed the longing in her heart a little, his blood tingling as she caught her lip with her teeth and flicked a quick glance toward where he and Kitt sat at the bar.

"Ahh." Kitt nodded. "I see. How do you even pick 'em?"

"Trade secret, Rover." He smiled at the woman, dropped her a wink and tossed a pretzel into his mouth.

"I really wish you'd stop calling me that."

James arched an eyebrow. "Do you *really* want to go with that particular choice of words, Kitt?"

"Shit." Kitt held up his hands. "You know that's not what I meant. Stop being so literal." He scowled and pivoted his stool back to the bar. "Remind me again why I hang out with you?"

"Because of this," James said, with another stroke to the woman's longing to sing, to throw caution aside and climbed up onto the stage.

She looked over her shoulder again toward the bar, toward him and Kitt.

Good girl. Good...

With a quick word in her date's ear, she walked over to the bar and rested her elbows on it, right beside James. "Can I get an ice water please?" she asked the barkeeper.

The barkeeper nodded and went to work.

"Thirsty?" James asked, reaching for another pretzel.

She let out a wobbly chuckle and tucked a strand of brown hair behind her ear. "No. Yes. Sorta."

He could feel her heart racing as she gave the stage a glance over her shoulder.

"You going to treat us all to a song?" He danced the pretzel over the back of his knuckles before tossing it into his mouth. "Belt out a tune? I was just saying to Rover here," he clapped a hand on Kitt's shoulder, "I feel a need to hear some Bon Jovi."

Her eyebrows lifted. "'Livin' on a Prayer'?"

"My favorite." He squeezed Kitt's shoulder with a grin. "This one here likes that old song from the '70s, 'Were-wolves of London'."

Kitt growled.

The woman chewed her bottom lip again and gave the karaoke stage another glance. James's blood tingled. "I'd love to get up there and sing," she said, as if sharing a profound secret. "But..."

I'm not brave enough. And what if I can't sing it as well as I do in the shower? Her thoughts tickled at James. *And what if my date laughs at—*

"Your water." The barkeeper placed a tall, beading glass in front of her on the bar, and she startled.

"But...?" James prodded. Two words. All he needed to hear were two simple words.

She shrugged and took a sip, studying the stage in the mirrored wall. "I'm not that good. At least, I don't think I am. I wish..."

James smiled. Warmth began to spread through him. His blood didn't just tingle, it rushed through his veins like liquid sunlight mixed with lightning. "You wish what?"

Her eyes met his in the mirror and she caught her bottom lip again. "I wish I was brave enough to not care if I don't sound like Adele, y'know? I wish I could just say to hell with what everyone thinks and go up there and have fun. And I wish, if I did, that I could actually surprise myself and sound amazing."

"Just those three wishes, eh?" James danced another pretzel over his knuckles and winked at her. "I like it. Done."

He nodded his head once—and released the rush.

The woman drew in a swift breath, held it for an eternity, and then slapped her hands on the bar, eyes shining. "Y'know what? To hell with being scared. I'm going to do it!"

"You're going to get up there and sing?" Kitt asked.

She grinned, slapped the bar again and nodded. "Yep. I'm going to go up there, sing 'Living on a Prayer' and have fun. Who cares, right? I don't." She frowned, as if contemplating what she'd said, and then laughed. "I truly don't!"

With another quick gulp of water, she spun on her heel and almost skipped through the crowd to where her date stood, watching her. Flinging her arms around his neck, she smacked an enthusiastic kiss on his mouth, and then hurried up the ramp to the karaoke MC's station.

"So are you responsible for—" Kitt started, but James silenced him with a finger.

"Shhh, mate," James whispered, riding the tsunami of giddy emotion. "Let me just savor this for a moment."

"Y'know you've lost your American accent, right?"

James didn't care. He closed his eyes, breathed in deeply, and readied himself for the rush of the third wish.

"You sound like a Brit again."

Music began to play, the distinctive introduction of Bon Jovi's seminal '80s classic.

The first word, her first note, hit him. Slammed into him. Flowed through him. Made every molecule in both his solid and ethereal forms frenzied.

The rush of the wish fulfilled.

"Oh yeah." If he still smoked, he'd light up. But it had been almost a thousand years and he wasn't going to start again. "Oh yeah," he repeated on a murmur.

"Yeah." Kitt chuckled, twisting on his stool back to the bar. "I guess that answers the question whether *you're* responsible for her getting up there."

James smiled, eyes still closed.

The woman sang, her voice pure and strong and incredible. Sure, he may have given it a little tweak for the sake of her longing, but she had the natural talent. Would she ever sing karaoke again? He had no clue. That wasn't his concern. Their interaction was done, finished, and he was okay with that.

Another of his kind may have extracted a price, a hidden condition to the covenant before granting her wishes, as he himself had been known to do, but for tonight, for these three wishes...

"You really are feeling generous tonight," Kitt said, a note of approval and awe in his voice.

"Sometimes the world needs a reminder it's not all hell in a handcart." James opened his eyes and watched in the mirror as the woman sang up a storm on the stage. Joy and delight radiated from her, sweetening the rush still flowing through him. On the dance floor stood her date, the musclebound firefighter gazing up at her with the dopiest smile of utter adoration.

James reached for his gin and tonic and held it out to Kitt in a relaxed toast. "To the rush of being a good guy."

Kitt laughed and chinked his glass to James's. "To good guys. Even if few humans know we are."

James winked at the wolf shifter. "Even then."

They grinned and swallowed the rest of their drinks in one go.

"What's with the changing accents?" Kitt asked, wiping at the residue of Scotch on his lips with the back of his hand. "Most of the time you sound British, and occasionally like you're from New Zealand, but I've noticed when you interact with some people, you sound American. And the other day you were talking to someone on the phone and sounded like you were from South Africa. Then a month ago, you were muttering to yourself in the lunch room and sounded Middle Eastern."

James snorted. "Did I? I must have been tired that day."

Kitt lifted an eyebrow.

"When I need to sound American, I sound American. When I need to sound South African, I sound South African. You see where I'm going with this? My place of origin—I'm talking thousands and thousands and *thousands* of years ago—is the Middle East, so that explains that one, but I spent quite a substantial amount of my existence here amongst mankind in the UK before I moved to LA, so it's sort of become my default accent."

Kitt narrowed his eyes. "There's a lot of secrets going on under that flippant persona of yours, Hastin."

James laughed. "You could say that about every one of us bastards working at Guarded Souls." He moved his attention to the woman now singing Adele's "Rolling in the Deep" on the karaoke stage. She was doing an amazing job, and her date was still gazing at her with rapt attention.

Narrowing his focus on the firefighter's emotions and thoughts, James chuckled. The man was head over heels in love. Her courage to get up and sing had been the final push for his romantic heart.

James closed his eyes, savoring the final waves of the rush. Like the last glimpses of light from the sun as it sank behind the horizon, the final rush flared stronger and more intense, and for a split second he was nothing but elemental force. And then the rush was over. Finished.

Sated, he opened his eyes and let out a long sigh.

"Does it ever piss you off?" Kitt asked. "Not getting any of the credit when you do something like this?" He indicated the singing woman with a slight tilt of his head.

"Something like this..." James smiled. "I do something like this for the rush."

"That good?"

"You have no idea."

Kitt chuckled. "If the expression on your face when she first started to sing was any indication, I think I do. You looked like you were about to blow your load."

James grinned, plucked a pretzel out of thin air and studied its perfection for a second. "Clearly, Rover, you've never seen me just as I'm about to blow my—"

"And I'm eternally grateful for that simple truth," Kitt cut in. "I like you, Genie Boy, but not that much."

"Genie Boy?"

Kitt flashed white teeth at him. "You call me Rover, I call you Genie Boy."

James held aloft his empty glass. "I'll drink to that." It filled to the brim with fresh gin and tonic, at the same moment Kitt's filled with Scotch.

"Ah, now see?" Kitt raised his primed glass. "*This* is why I hang out with you."

"Free booze?"

"Free booze." Kitt tapped his glass to James's. "Cheers."

James laughed. "So, Rover, now I've had my fun, wanna tell me what's the deal with the mysterious text messages you keep getting from—"

James's cellphone vibrated to life in his waistcoat's inside pocket, at the exact moment Kitt's phone did the same on the bar top.

"Message from the boss," Kitt said, frowning at his phone screen even as a wave of relief rolled from him so potent, James felt it. If the text hadn't been from Kade, James would have pushed the issue. Something was troubling the wolf shifter, something dark enough to put him on edge. "He wants us in the office ASAP."

Pulling his own phone from his waistcoat, James read the message on the screen: *Will the wolf and the djinn please get their hairy asses into work pronto? Got an emergency job and I need both of you.*

"Okay, I'll accept your arse is hairy," he said, throwing Kitt a grin, "but mine?"

Kitt snorted, shoving his phone into his pocket as he straightened from the barstool. "Did you drive here?"

"Ah, Rover, you're too adorable for your own hairy-arsed good sometimes." James squeezed Kitt's shoulder. "Ready?"

Kitt's eyes widened. "No. No! Don't you—"

James clicked his fingers.

"—dare," Kitt groaned. He scowled at the Guarded Souls' entry foyer, before turning the scowl on James. "I hate it when you do that."

James grinned. "I know, Rover. I know."

Kitt dragged his hand down his face, shook his head then his shoulders, and let out a ragged breath. "One of these days, I'm going to shift form and cock my leg on—"

"You two took your time." Kade appeared at the door leading into the security firm's offices, his expression as enigmatic as ever. "Hurry up. This is a tricky one."

Without another word, he turned and walked away.

James flicked Kitt a look. "Smell anything fishy?"

"Ha ha." Kitt rolled his eyes, and then drew a slow breath. "Although whoever the tricky client is, she's wearing Chanel No. 5 perfume."

"Why do you know what Chanel No. 5 perfume smells like?"

Kitt dropped him a wink and strode after Kade.

"Fair enough." James followed. Regardless of the fact it was almost midnight, when the boss said it was time to work, it was time to work.

Beyond the quiet entry foyer, Guarded Souls was silent.

Individual offices and meeting rooms sat dark except for Kade's at the end of a wide corridor. White light spilled from the partly opened door, the low murmur of his deep voice rumbling on the air like distant thunder as Kitt stepped into the room.

James threw his own office a quick glance as he walked past. What were the chances his peace lily was still alive? Feathers was probably making certain it was; the angel had a thing for keeping plants going even when water didn't come anywhere near their roots. James himself rarely used the space, with its state-of-the-art office equipment and luxurious, modern furniture, preferring to do any official paperwork either at home or wherever he happened to find himself when it needed to be done.

Plus, there was the fact Nim had foolishly said to him she'd do anything for a Reuben sandwich, and he'd granted her wish. The wiccan was now doing his paperwork for a month. (She really did need to rethink how loosely she threw the W-word around in the lunchroom.)

As far as work went, being on the Guarded Souls payroll was pretty cushy; most of the clients engaging the agency's protection and security services were extremely rich and, in the majority of cases, more paranoid about being under threat than they were any kind of actual target. But it did make for some interesting work hours. Not really a problem for James—or any of those employed by Kade. Given that none of the protection staff were human, common human hours weren't an issue. But the ancient vampire did like to maintain a human façade for the firm, which meant keeping normal business hours for the ancillary staff.

Being called in for a job at midnight, though? That was...different.

Even more different? Kade using the term *tricky*.

In the years that James had been a Guarded Souls member, he'd only ever seen Kade stressed once. And that was when the entire security team, including Kade himself, almost—

"...getting tired of being treated like a fragile victim here."

James froze at the female voice coming from Kade's office. His heart smashed up into his throat.

Fark.

He knew that voice, that Northern English accent. That fierce confidence.

It's not her. Can't be. She's in London. You know that. She's—

"Because I'm not," the woman went on, the calm challenge in her voice more familiar than his own reflection. "Fragile. Or a victim. I merely heard something I wasn't meant to."

Yep. It was her.

Shite. Why in the name of all things British was Tahlee Hope here in LA?

Bracing himself for what was about to happen, James stepped into Kade's office and smiled at the woman he'd left three years ago. "Hey, Hope. Long time no speak to."

AT WHAT POINT in her life had she done something so heinous that she deserved to be kicked in the arse by karma like this?

And more to the point, what would the other two men in the room do if she stood up and unceremoniously kneed James Hastin in the nuts?

"Hello, James." She bestowed a wide smile on the tall,

lanky man leaning against the doorframe, letting him see her teeth. "You're still alive? Huh. Who knew?"

James—the bastard—ducked his head and gave her a sheepish grin. He hadn't changed much. Still looked like the embodiment of mischief and sexual rapture all wrapped up in one delicious package.

"You've been well?" he asked.

"Wait." The towering man with the dark hair who'd first met her at the police station an hour ago held up his hands, his green eyes swinging back and forth between her and James. "What's going on here?"

James did that sheepish chuckle of his that had always reduced her to a quivering mess of arousal and adoration. Flipping hell. She wasn't going to let that happen now, not after what he did to her. "I knew Hope when I was still living in London," he said.

Living in London.

Huh. More like living in her flat. Sleeping in her bed.

Agitated, she reached for the small pendant normally hanging on a fine gold chain around her neck, but it wasn't there. She'd left it in her hotel room, tucked in the room's safe along with her passport, before heading to the Getty Museum.

Bugger.

"Define *knew*," said the man who'd arrived in the office a few moments before James, arching an eyebrow. Kitt Newton? Was that his name? She'd been too busy arguing with Guarded Souls' owner—Kade Somethingorother—about whether she really needed protection or not to pay attention when introductions were made. Uncharacteristic of her, to be sure. Normally her mind was a steel trap on details like that.

"Do you know what?" She rose to her feet, shaking her

head. "As I explained to Mr..." She waved her hand at Tall-Dark-and-Brooding.

"Just Kade is fine," TDB provided, a half smile tugging at one corner of his mouth.

"As I explained to Mr. *Just* Kade before you arrived, I'm fine. I don't need protection. I just need to go home. And by home, I mean London."

To the flat she and James used to share a different life-time ago.

Sheesh.

The prickling caress on her profile told her James was studying her. She'd always known when he was looking at her. It was as if her body was intrinsically tuned into his. When he'd been close, she'd just felt...more alive. It had been a wonderful feeling when they'd been together. The emptiness, the betrayal replacing it when he disappeared three years ago? That had been a flipping crappy feeling.

"What's the story, Kade?" James wandered into the room, dropped himself on the chair beside the one where she'd been sitting and dumped his heels on Kade's desk, crossing his ankles. "Why does Hope need protection?"

Her heart quickened at the sound of his voice saying her last name. In the years she'd known him, in the months they'd been together, he'd rarely called her anything but her last name. She liked it back then. Now...

Kade's direct stare made her want to fidget. "Please, Ms. Hope," he said, voice smooth and deep and calm. So calm, like a bottomless lake undisturbed by wind or life. "The situation you've found yourself in is worrying. And dangerous. Let us pro— *Help* you."

She narrowed her eyes. He'd stopped himself from saying "protect". That was a good sign. He'd already identi-fied she didn't like the notion of being vulnerable or dependent on anyone. Of course, he'd *also* hired a lying sod like James Hastin, so she'd reserve final judgement of Kade for a while.

"Wait wait wait." James's feet thudded to the floor, and he snapped his stare from her to Kade and back again. "Dangerous? Hope's in danger?"

Rolling her eyes, she sighed and shook her head. She did not need him going all caveman on her. "I'm not in danger, James. I overheard something, reported it to the police, and now they feel I need a security detail, which is why I'm here. And come to think of it, why are *you* here? The last time we saw each other," *when you walked out of the restaurant where we were having dinner a second after I told you I love you, never to return,* "you were a dog groomer."

"A dog..." Kitt Newton gaped at James for a second, and then threw back his head. Tahlee's lips twitched. Damn, his laugh sounded almost like a howl. "A dog groomer?" He grinned. "That's priceless. Next time I need a haircut I'll give you a call, Jimmy Boy."

James pointed his finger at Kitt, his smile savage. "Be my guess, Rover. While I'm at it, how 'bout I give that pretty gray fur of yours a dye job?"

Tahlee frowned. What?

"Enough," Kade murmured.

James chuckled, smile turning smug. Kitt shook his head, even as he ran a quick hand through his ash-blond hair.

Tahlee frowned deeper. She didn't know what she'd expected when Kade had arrived at the police station, but it wasn't this. She'd had experiences with security firms before—she was an investigative journalist for London's biggest newspaper, after all. Her byline came with clout and made some people—influential, significant people—nervous. She'd had more than one death threat against her back home.

But Guarded Souls wasn't like any of the previous agencies.

For starters, none of them had employed the bastard who broke my heart.

"This is all very weird and entertaining," she said, shoving the thought aside. She'd deal with James later. She'd get him alone somehow and tear strips off him, but for the moment... "But I really would like to just go home. Or even back to my hotel room."

Three sets of stares focused on her. She met James's for a second, her stupid pulse quickening at just how green his eyes still were, before turning to Kade. Of the three men, the owner of Guarded Souls seemed the most... grown-up. "I know the police insist I'm in danger, but the men I overheard didn't know I was there. As far as I know, they still don't. So why would they—"

"What men?" James sat up straighter. Impossible as it was, he seemed to suddenly look bigger. Menacing. Which was ridiculous. Tall, rangy James Hastin was far from menacing or dangerous.

She'd fallen for James Hastin because of his goofy, relaxed approached to life. His quick smile and wit. Dangerous, menacing men did not push her buttons.

And yet, right now...

"Tell me about the men." He narrowed those green eyes at her. "What exactly have you gotten yourself into, Hope?"

"This is..." She let out a ragged breath. "Can't I just...I don't know, buy a gun? I know how to shoot one. I completed a gun-use course for an article I wrote, and I can get one from a Kmart or a Walmart, or some other kind of mart, yes?"

"Hope." James reached out and closed his fingers around hers, and her heart skipped a beat. Damn it. "Tell me what's going on."

She looked down at their hands. Studied the way they fit together, remembered how many times they'd held hands at the movies, or walking through Green Park, or doing the grocery shopping together at the Waitrose on the corner near their flat in Wimbledon.

Withdrawing her fingers from his, she lifted her head and met his worried eyes.

You don't get to be worried about me anymore, James Hastin.

Pain flickered over his face, as if he'd heard her angry thought.

"Hope..." he murmured, searching her eyes.

She pressed a hand to her face, and let out a sigh. "I wish..."

He pulled in a sharp breath.

So did Kade and Kitt.

Dropping her hand, she reached for her pendant again, remembered she wasn't wearing it, and sat back in her seat, plucking at the fraying strands of denim at the knees of her favorite jeans instead. "Okay, fine. I'm here in LA on a holiday."

"Translation," James regarded her, a small grin playing with his lips, "Hope has her nose on a story and followed it here to LA."

Bastard. He knew her so well.

Too well?

There'd be no point fudging the truth. Not with James in the room. Sure, she'd been able to dance around the real reason for trip to LA with the cops and Kade, but James *always* had a way of knowing when she was being truthful. It was incredible. Freeing, even. A week after meeting him in a pub in Piccadilly, she'd given up on the notion of treating him like she treated everyone else—as if they were the enemy, not to be trusted—and opened up to him in ways she never had with anyone else. It had been exhilarating and wonderful and even empowering.

And three years later, he left. Without a word or reason.

"Yes, I have my nose on a story." She twisted her lips at him, and then returned her attention to Kade. "One about a UK politician." A *corrupt* UK politician. The likely future Prime Minister of the UK. "So as a consequence, I snuck into the gala fundraiser at the Getty Museum tonight...or should that be last night? I don't even know what time it is...12:47 am? Wow. Anyway, I snuck into the fundraiser where he was a guest speaker and surreptitiously followed his advisor around for a little while until, somehow, I found myself in the men's toilet."

James laughed.

Tahlee smiled. She couldn't help it. Whenever James laughed, it made her smile.

Stop it. You're angry with him. Furious, in fact.

Pulling a slow breath, she tuned out the bastard and met Kade's unwavering gaze. "I suspected I'd been spotted by the event's security, so I hurried through the closest unlocked door."

Kade's expression didn't change. "Which happened to be the men's bathroom?"

James chuckled again.

She bit the inside of her cheek to stop herself from beaming at him with pride. "I went into a cubicle, climbed up onto the toilet seat, and was preparing to either wait it out there for a few minutes or get busted. That's when two men walked in, talking to each other."

"Rourke's aide and the unknown man," Kade said.

"Rourke's aide and an unknown man," Tahlee confirmed.

"Rourke? As in Maximillian Rourke?" Kitt spoke up.

Tahlee started. She'd actually forgotten he was there. Which was unnerving, given she'd made a living out of being aware of people constantly.

"Who the hell's Maximillian Rourke?" James asked.

Kitt frowned at him. "Really? Well, that clears up a question I've had about the man for a while."

James frowned in return. "What question's that?"

"Whether you had anything to do with his meteoric rise or not."

Tahlee blinked. Why would anyone think a dog groomer from London had something to do with the infamous American businessman's ascent in politics?

Confusion crossed James's face. No man had any right looking that sexy when confused. "I have no clue who Rourke is, so it's definitely a not. Who is he?"

"Maximillian Rourke," Kade said, sliding his attention to James, "is an importer/exporter, billionaire, and currently on the fast track to becoming a future Presidential nominee."

Tahlee grunted. That barely scratched the surface of the rumors and conjecture surrounding Maximillian Rourke. He was painted as a golden-boy hero by some media outlets, and a narcissistic and unscrupulous villain by others. If Tahlee lived in the US, Rourke would be a prime target for her journalistic instincts, which itched like crazy whenever he popped up in the news back home.

But her sights were fixed on Glenn Simmons, the

corrupt British minister seemingly hellbent on destroying the UK's relationship with Europe...and damn near the rest of the free world.

James shook his head. "Nope. I had nothing to do with Rourke's rise. Some other gen—" He flicked Tahlee a glance. "*Genius*. Not me. I wasn't the genius responsible."

Kitt chuckled. "In that case, Christen owes me a hundred bucks. He bet you did."

James laughed. "Clearly the Norseman and I need to have a chat."

Kitt grinned. "Hey, we all know about your part in William Shatner's—"

"Enough," Kade said again.

Kitt closed his mouth and settled back in his chair, amber eyes turned back to Tahlee. James locked his lips—twitching with that sheepish grin that always did stuff to Tahlee she never really understood, but loved all the same—and flicked away the invisible key.

"I apologize for my colleagues," Kade said, sliding them both unreadable looks before returning his attention to her. "They were at a karaoke bar when I called them in and..." He shrugged, leaving the rest of his sentence dangling.

Tahlee narrowed her eyes at Kade. Met his unblinking gaze. The mention of the karaoke bar was designed to distract. Of that she had little doubt, but from what? And why? Something was going on here. James at a karaoke bar? James couldn't sing to save himself. And referring to himself as a genius? He was glib and mischievous and funny, but he was rarely boastful.

And just what the flipping hell did William Shatner have to do with anything?

It was all very peculiar. Maybe she needed to look into it a little—

"What did you overhear Rourke's aide say, Ms. Hope?" Kade asked. Still calm radiated from him, as if he had all of eternity to wait for her response.

The detective she'd given her statement to had freaked out at what she'd overheard. Not visibly, but she'd inter-viewed enough people in her time to recognize the signs— eyes widening, swift intake of breath, reflex balling of a hand into a fist, minute stiffening of his muscles and straightening of his spine. Would the owner of Guarded Souls do the same?

And what about James? How's he going to react, learning what you overheard?

How James reacted didn't matter.

Remember the time that guy felt you up in the pub in Covent Gardens? Remember what he did when James appeared? Remember how the guy took one look at him, just one, and burst into apologetic tears, damn near dropping to his knees, groveling for mercy...

"What did you overhear, Hope?"

She sighed at James's low question. The concern in his voice played merry-hell with her resolve to ignore him.

Huh, you haven't been able to ignore James Hastin from the first second you saw him. It's as if he's the light and you're the hungry, thirsty moth.

"Tahlee?"

Her heart thumped into her throat at the sound of him saying her name. Her *first* name. Damn him.

Letting out another sigh, she tilted her chin. Forced her focus to stay on Kade and Kitt, even as she remembered the glimpses of the short bald man she'd seen through the tiny gap around the toilet cubicle door. "He said 'make sure she stays gone. For good. If Rourke sees her face on television again it won't just be *her* tongue torn out, do you understand?'"

Rourke's aide had said more, but it had been so low and mumbled, Tahlee couldn't hear it correctly. It sounded like gibberish. But whatever he had muttered, it made her flesh crawl. For the brief second Rourke's aide uttered those indistinct, possibly foreign words, inexplicable terror ripped through her, unlike any she'd ever experienced before. As if her very soul understood them and feared them. As if every horror in the world, every horror in *every* world, had somehow been condensed into a single moment, and was now slithering up her spine, into her ears, her mouth, her nose, her eyes.

She'd pressed her hand to her mouth, silencing the scream tearing its way up from her soul before it could burst free.

That infinitesimal movement, though...

She'd crouched on the toilet seat, staring at the closed cubicle door, staring at its unlocked latch. Waiting for the door to swing open. For Rourke's aide to reach in and grab her, tear her tongue—

"Well, that's not good."

James's calm voice jerked her back to the room. Heart racing, she met his gaze.

Just hug him. Press your body to his, your cheek to his chest, and hug him. He'll take the fear away. You know he will. He'll—

"No," she said, her own voice husky. "It isn't. I don't know who the *she* is, otherwise I would have warned her. Whoever she is, *she* needs to be protected. Not me."

An unreadable light flickered in James's green eyes and he straightened from his chair. "I'll be back."

He walked from the room. Just like that.

Tahlee blinked.

"Kitt," Kade said.

"On it." Kitt jolted to his feet and followed James.

Tahlee blinked. Again. "What..." She frowned at Kade. "Okay, something weird is going on here. What is it?"

Kade studied her, expression as calm and enigmatic as his eyes. "Your insistence you aren't in danger, Ms. Hope."

"Really?" She crossed her arms and arched an eyebrow. "You're very good at misdirection, Mr. *Just* Kade, but I'm not buying it anymore."

Eyes holding hers, he smiled—and the world erupted in a gush of joy and light and wonder. Just like that, she felt better.

Wow.

"Would you like a cup of tea?" He straightened to his feet, buttoning his suit jacket. "I've got Lady Grey, Earl Grey, and English breakfast." He made his way toward the room's small but state-of-the-art kitchenette. "Chai, jasmine, Darjeeling."

"Where's James gone?"

He paused, hand poised at the handle of an electric kettle.

"And why did you send—"

"Nothing."

Tahlee gasped as James strode back into the room, Kitt following. A scowl darkened James's face. Exasperation did the same to Kitt's.

"Can't find a bloody thing." James's British accent wavered, and for a moment, Tahlee couldn't place where he sounded like he came from. "Whatever's going on with this Rourke dude's aide, I can't detect—" He stopped, his eyes touching hers for a second. "I can't find anything on Google."

Kitt grunted, dumping himself into one of the chairs in the room. "Google needs to calm the hell down and take a breath, before Google slips up big time."

"Bite me, Rover."

Kitt bared his teeth at James.

The base of Tahlee's spine itched. When the base of her spine itched, it usually meant something unexpected and nefarious was happening. Something she could sink her journalist's teeth into. But what exactly would be stirring those instincts now?

The fact James is here? And seems to exude some kind of mesmerizing power and strength you've never noticed in him before?

James—the James she'd fallen in love with—had never seemed so flustered and agitated and...and...dangerous.

James? Dangerous?

Her heart thumped faster in her chest. She needed to get her arse back to London ASAP. Or sooner.

No one back in the UK, save for her editor, knew she'd flown to the US, and there was no one waiting for her, but still...she had a story to write, damn it.

Clearing his throat, Kade lifted the kettle and filled it from the tap. "I'm making Ms. Hope a cup of tea."

"Darjeeling," James said. "Black. Strong. Two sugars."

Of course he remembers how you like your tea. She ground her teeth, reaching for her absent necklace again. Damn him.

Kade regarded him. "I've had a thought."

"Watch out. That can be painful."

Leaning his hip against the bench, Kade folded his arms, a smile tugging at one side of his mouth. "I was going to assign you *and* Kitt to this job, Jimmy Boy, but I've changed my mind."

James narrowed his eyes, even as Kitt raised his dark eyebrows. "What do you mean, 'changed your mind'?"

"My gut tells me," Kade went on, his unblinking gaze moving to Tahlee for a heartbeat before returning to James, "that Ms. Hope doesn't need two of my crew protecting her. Not when there's no hope in hell *you'll* ever let anything happen to her. Am I right, Hastin?"

James's Adam's apple slid up and down his smooth throat. "What are you saying, boss?"

Kade smiled, his stare locked on James. "I'm saying I'm assigning *you*, James, to the job of looking after Guarded Souls' newest client, Tahlee Hope. Only you. Until I deem it necessary, you will be her constant companion. Twenty-four seven. Do I make myself clear?"

James pulled in a deep, shaky breath.

Tahlee did the same. Flipping hell.

2

Philips inspected the nails of his right hand. He always appreciated a good manicure. Made the times he needed to really look closely at his hands far more palatable. "What do you mean, you can't find her?"

"She's...just gone, sir. There's no sign of her."

Lowering his hand to his desk, Philips drummed his nails—short and buffed to a low shine—on the rich mahogany. "How did you let this happen?"

"I...I..."

He exhaled, lifting his hand again. Silence filled the room, the sudden loss of the rapid tattoo of his nails deafening. He moved his focus to the simpering grunt in front of his desk. "I? I?"

The grunt trembled. As he should. With the news he'd just delivered, he knew what was about to happen.

As William Shakespeare had been fond of saying— loudly and drunkenly, sometimes—there was a time and place for shooting the messenger.

"Wherever she's gone, she's no longer detectable," the grunt said.

"Shielded, you mean?" A cold fist twisted in Philips's gut. "Warded?"

"Maybe. I think so. I tracked her to the cop station. Watched her leave with a tall man. I hooked into her, like you taught me, but when she climbed into a car with him, she..." The grunt shuffled his feet and rubbed at the back of his burly neck.

"What?" The cold fist twisted some more. A chilly dread seeped into Philips's bones. This is what he got for trusting something as important as this to a wannabe with only a trickle of ability. "She what?"

The grunt swallowed. "It's like she just disappeared. From existence. I followed the car as long as I could, but lost it in traffic."

"In traffic. At almost one am, there was traffic? Enough traffic to lose sight of a car you were following?"

"Y-yes. The tall guy drove fast."

Raising his eyebrows, Philips sat back in his seat. "Is that so? Describe him."

"Tall. Dark hair. Black suit, black shirt. Maybe a black waistcoat."

"The car?"

"Black. Some kind of German sedan. The one with four rings on the grill."

"So, the woman who overheard me discussing tearing the tongue from another woman's mouth went to the police, left with an unknown man driving one of probably thousands of Audis in this town, and now cannot be located via any...*means* you've tried?"

The grunt's head jiggled on his neck like a goddamn bobblehead on crack.

"Did you think to speak to the detective she talked to? Maybe ask for her name? Or the name of the man she left with?"

"Umm..."

Holding up his hand again, Philips reached for the phone on his desk. "What police station did she leave from?"

"West LA Community Police Station, on Butler Avenue."

Stabbing out a number, Philips held the grunt's gaze. Refused to release it.

Refused to let the imbecile blink.

"Hello," he said when the connection was made. "I need to know the name of all the detectives on shift at the West LA Community Police Station in the last twelve hours."

Returning the phone to its cradle, he raised his eyebrows at the grunt. "Now, that wasn't so hard, was it."

"I'm sorry, Mr. Philips. Sometimes I forget about doing things that way."

Philips pulled open the top drawer of his desk, withdrew the Kimber 1911 pistol inside and shot the grunt in the middle of the forehead.

An uncouth way of dealing with a problem, to be sure, but sometimes it just wasn't worth the spell to do the job.

SHE WAS GOING to kill him.

Well, not literally. It was tricky to kill a djinn, the act required a certain procedure and spell, and she didn't have the skillset, or the knowledge he *was* a djinn, but still...

At the soft click of the door closing behind Kade and Kitt, James turned back to Tahlee.

She arched an eyebrow at him, crossed her arms and slung her leg over her knee. "You bastard."

"I can explain." He couldn't. Not even close. How could he possibly explain why he'd vanished from her life mere minutes after she'd professed the most profound, significant, powerful feeling a human could have for another?

"Okay then." She swung her foot a little, her eyes locked on him.

He shifted on his seat. Swallowed at the lump in his throat. Rubbed at the back of his neck.

"Oh, you mean, you *can* explain, but not today?" Her lips twisted. "Or is it that you can, but you're just not *going* to?"

He ducked his head and gave her a sheepish smile. "Just...can't."

Her eyes closed for a heartbeat, and she let out a soft sigh. "Like the time in the pub at Covent Gardens?"

Ah, the infamous 'pub incident', when he'd reduced the guy who'd felt Tahlee up to a gibbering mess with a single djinn-powered look. How he'd escaped explaining *that* one, he didn't know. Some higher power had been smiling on him that night.

Or maybe it had been the spectacular dip-and-kiss move he'd performed, reducing her to a moaning puddle of sexual arousal, immediately after confronting the guy?

When it came to distracting her, he'd been a master.

Ha. Master. You're a comedian, Jimmy Boy.

Tahlee's lips twisted more. "I still don't understand what happened on that dance floor."

And she never would if he had any say in it. Even now,

what had transpired left him unnerved. Impressed with his own skill, but also unnerved.

Smiling, he threaded his hands behind his head. "I see you're still into making life hell for wankers."

She barked out a laugh. "That's very perceptive and honest of you to call yourself a wanker, James."

"I was referring to the politician you followed from London."

Her lips curled in a smug smile.

He grinned, even as a sharp longing stabbed at his heart. He'd missed her. So much. Every day, in fact. Had spent endless hours and minutes convincing himself the aching pang would one day go away.

That day had yet to come. But it would.

It had to.

And now you're going to be in her company twenty-four seven for who knows how long. Remember what happened the last time you were in this situation?

"So what happens now?"

He filled his lungs at her question and let it out in a shaky laugh. "I'm going to take you somewhere safe."

"My hotel? London?" Biting delight danced in her eyes. "Walmart?"

"A safe house."

A slight frown tugged at her dark eyebrows. "Not your place?"

"No." No way was he strong enough to take Tahlee back to his place. For starters, she'd scoff at his bachelor-pad décor (granting wishes to drunken CEOs in bars paid off sometimes), and secondly, he'd have to move out the second she left his life again. Anytime he'd look at anything she'd touched... "The safe house is warded, so no one will be able to locate you, no matter how clever they are."

"Warded? You mean guarded?"

Shite. "Yeah. Guarded. High-tech security. I think it's called the Ward System."

The Ward System? What the fuck was he going on about? And how quickly could Nim or Christen or...or...hell, *any* other Guarded Souls team member get to the safe house and plant some kind of high-tech-looking security boxes?

Tahlee narrowed her eyes. "There are so many things you're not telling me, James Hastin."

She wasn't wrong.

She shook her head. "I don't like it."

He didn't, either. Back in London, he'd rarely kept anything from her. Apart from the fact he was an ageless djinn trapped in the world of man, and that James Hastin wasn't his real name, or even his *first* fake name, and—

"Let's get going." He almost leaped to his feet. "It'll take a while to drive to the safe house, and I'll have to get gas on the way."

"James."

He moved to the door.

"James."

Grabbing the doorknob, he threw her a smile over his shoulder. "We'll swing by your hotel and grab your stuff."

"James."

Shite.

Stopping, he let out another ragged breath and leaned back against the wall beside the door. "Okay. You've got questions. That's only fair."

She sat motionless, her eyes searching his.

They were as beautiful as he remembered. As beautiful

as they'd always been. Hazel green with emerald chips, and direct and challenging as ever. Her lashes were as long and thick and as dark as her hair, and for the first time, he realized she wasn't wearing her glasses. He'd always liked her glasses. She'd had a quirky little habit of pulling them from her face and swinging them around by one stem when she was feeling playful.

She wouldn't be swinging them around now. There was nothing playful about the way she regarded him. In her beautiful eyes, a world of hurt and anger swam.

"Hit me with them," he said. This wasn't going to be pretty. If she didn't hate him already, she would soon.

She swallowed, eyebrows dipping. "Why?"

He didn't need to ask what she meant.

Why had he taken off a few minutes after she'd told him she loved him, never to have any connection with her again?

That soft, single-word question tore at him, ripped him apart. But the wretched pain, the acrid guilt that word awoke in him, was nothing compared to what could've happened if he'd stayed.

If only he could tell her.

"Because I'm a coward," he said.

The air cracked with the swift intake of her breath. Whatever she'd been expecting him to say, it wasn't that.

"Bullshit." She shook her head, jaw clenching. "You're a lot of things, James, but a coward?" She shook her head again.

What should he do?

There were a number of untold things he *could* do...if he wanted to unleash his true power on her.

And what would that *do? You know all about cause and*

effect. If you removed yourself from her memory, her soul, what would happen when she—

"I wish I'd never met you," she said quietly.

The room turned cold, artic. His breath crushed his lungs.

And then the tingle began. Deep in his core. The rush...

"You what?"

She scrunched up her face and shook her head a third time. "You destroyed me, James. I've never loved anyone before, but I loved *you*. And I told you, I bared my soul to you, and you excused yourself, said you needed to go to the bathroom. You were always one for mischief, so I thought you were having a lark, but you never came back. I sat at that table, in that restaurant, for I don't know how long, waiting for you to come back...and you never did. I told you I loved you, and you disappeared," she clicked her fingers, "just like that. But what really does my head in is... I was *certain* you felt the same for me."

He swallowed the dry planet in his throat.

"I was sure you loved me back," she continued, her voice steady and calm and all the more cutting for it. "And then you vanished." The shadow of pain darkened her eyes. "I wish..."

Don't say it. Please don't say—

"Hey, Hastin." The door swung open, and Kitt stuck his head through the gap. "Nathanial's got the safe house ready for you."

Tahlee straightened to her feet. "I'm going back to London."

James straightened. "No."

"No?"

Kitt cleared his throat. "Hastin is correct. It seems your

presence in the men's bathroom didn't go as unnoticed, as you believed, Ms. Hope. Kade just took a call from the detective you spoke to. Your room at the Residence Inn has been," he flicked James a quick glance, "trashed."

James curled his fists. His quick jump into the temporal plane earlier hadn't revealed any threat to Tahlee; no otherworldly threads had linked back to Rourke's aide, nor any human ones.

He'd almost believed her presence in the men's toilet had been missed.

Clearly that wasn't the case.

"Trashed?" Shock flittered over Tahlee's face, followed by irritation. Not fear, not panic, just anger and frustration. "Great. My laptop was there. Excellent. There goes all the work I'd done on Simmons."

"You don't back it up?"

She raised her eyes at Kitt. "To the Cloud? You're kidding, right? I don't trust the Cloud."

Tahlee didn't trust anyone or anything.

Except James. She'd told him that one night, stretched out beside him in their bed, her bare leg slung across his bare thigh, her fingers playing with his right nipple, her breath warm on his chest. "*Trusting only makes you weak,*" she'd whispered. "*But I trust you, James. It's like you've been in my heart forever.*"

The confession had filled him with a dangerous level of joy. He'd responded by taking her to hitherto unknown heights of sexual pleasure.

He should have gotten out then and there.

He hadn't.

Tell Kitt to take her to the safe house. Give the wolf shifter the job of protecting Tahlee. Get her out of your life. Again. Before it's too late.

His gut clenched.

You know you have to. You know what almost happened before. What will *happen if you—*

He held out his hand to Tahlee. "C'mon, Hope. Let's get your arse to the safe house."

No way he was letting anyone else protect her. Even someone as capable as Kitt.

She studied his hand, and then frowned up at him. "Can we go via the hotel?"

"It's all good. I can rustle up some new PJs and whatnot for you."

Rustle. Ha, he'd never used that word before to describe the djinn procurement of...things.

An unreadable tension passed over her face and her hand moved to the middle of her chest before dropping back to her lap. "It's not..."

Kitt cleared his throat. "There was no laptop listed in the items found in the room, Ms. Hope."

"It's not my laptop. There's something..." She threw a frown at James again. "Else."

"We can do that."

"I don't think..." Uncertainty filled Kitt's voice.

James grinned at him. "It's all good, Rover. Don't stress."

Kitt raised his eyebrows.

"I've got it covered." And he did. The odds of the person or persons who'd tossed Tahlee's room coming back while they were there were slim, and if they did... well, James had ways of dealing with them. It'd make everyone's job easier if they *did* come back, in fact.

And if they do, you can take out some of your frustration on them before handing them over to the cops.

Tempting, but he couldn't let Tahlee see his true self,

his true power. Of course, that didn't mean he couldn't get physical—human style. It'd been a while since he'd gotten into an old-fashioned fist fight, to be sure, but he could still floor a man in one punch if needed, no djinn force required.

"Sure you don't want me to come along?" Kitt asked.

"He'll be okay." Kade appeared at the door. "I know he won't let anything happen to Ms. Hope."

James narrowed his eyes. The vampire's behavior was unusual. Like he was up to something. Although, to be fair, Kade was always up to something and rarely predictable. The only constant thing about Kade was the fact you never knew what was going on behind those piercing green eyes of his.

"Take the Jeep." Kade tossed a set of keys at James. "It'll be better in this case than that thing you normally get around in."

That thing you normally get around in being code for translocating at will, no car or bike or any other form of human transportation required.

Kitt chuckled.

James grimaced. Figures Kade would know he hadn't yet thought about how he'd get Tahlee to the safe house. The whole "stop for gas" thing had been a woeful attempt to appear as if Tahlee suddenly being back in his life meant nothing.

Of course, if Kade hadn't already tossed keys at him, James would have just...procured a traditional mode of transportation before he and Tahlee reached the Guarded Souls parking lot. A quick cough to hide the click and voila —a Harley. Or Ferrari.

Dipping into a mocking bow, he grinned at Kade. "Thank you, boss." He turned to Tahlee. "M'lady?"

"You don't get to call me that, Hastin."

"I like her, Jimmy Boy." Kitt chuckled again. "Whatever history there is between you, can you get it all settled? She'd been fun at the Guarded Souls Halloween party."

"You're a riot, Rover. A riot."

"Are you sure I can't go back to London?" Tahlee folded her arms. "I've got a goldfish with serious attitude holding down the fort back there. He'll keep me safe."

"Gary is still alive?"

A soft smile played with her lips. "Gary is still alive."

They'd bought Gary together at the Portobello Road markets. A month before he took off.

"Good for Gary." He grinned. "But no. You can't."

Her jaw bunched, and she let out a choppy breath. "You're going to be my undoing, James Hastin."

He chuckled, even as that old familiar pang hit his heart again. If only she knew the truth. "If it helps, I've gotten really good at putting the toilet seat down since you last knew me."

She snorted, rolling her eyes. "Yeah, like *that's* the reason I want to kill you. Let's go."

And with that, she strode past Kade and Kitt and out of Kade's office.

Kitt's lips twitched. Kade regarded him with an unblinking gaze. "Have fun."

Fun.

James's chest tightened. Fun wasn't really the word coming to mind.

Shite, he was in trouble.

∽

DUCKING under the police tape crisscrossing the door to her suite at the Residence Inn, James let out a soft whistle. "Well, whoever they were, you've got to give them points for a job well done."

Rolling her eyes, Tahlee began to duck beneath the tape as well.

"No, no." James bent at the waist, locking stares with her from the other side of the threshold, and shook his head. "You're staying there for a moment."

She straightened. "Really?"

He chuckled, his usual response to any scathing sarcasm she directed his way when they were together.

Together. What they weren't anymore.

Her throat thickened. "It's my room." She flicked the police tape with her fingers. "I'm coming in."

"Sure. Give me a sec first, though."

She rolled her eyes. "James, I don't think the bad guys are in there now, do you."

He grinned. "Say *bad guys* again."

"No." She hooked her fingers under the police tape.

"Just—" He halted her hand with his own. "Give me a moment. Please?"

She studied his face, his enigmatic expression. "Okay. You've got until I count to ten."

"Perfect." He turned to the room. Stood motionless.

Tahlee frowned at his back. "You're not going in?"

"Shh." He raised an index finger without looking at her.

"Fine. One, two, three, four."

He chuckled but didn't move.

"Five. Six." Crossing her arms beneath her breasts, she scowled. "Seven."

"Done." He half-turned and pulled the police tape up a few inches. "Come see what you can find."

Ducking under the tape, she stepped into her suite. Whoa, whoever had been in here truly had destroyed it. Nothing was right-side up. The generic hotel artworks had been pulled from the walls, the suite's furniture had been flipped, the cushions and pillows shredded, the sheets and blankets ripped from the bed and scattered.

Her clothes lay strewn all over the floor, as did what remained of the contents of her laptop and camera bags.

Shit.

What would have happened to her if she'd been here when they—whoever *they* were—had arrived?

Would she still be alive?

Pulling a steadying breath, she turned her attention back to James. She couldn't let him see she was rattled. "What was that about?"

Damn it, her voice shook. A little.

Please don't let him notice.

His eyebrows rose. "What?"

"Making me wait on the other side of the tape."

"Ah. I wanted to see if any bad guys jumped out at me."

"Ha ha."

He pulled a wounded pout. "You don't think I have my clients' safety in mind?"

"Seriously, what was that about?"

"I just...needed to get a vibe from the room."

"A vibe?" She narrowed her eyes. "You were less complicated when you were a dog groomer."

"But not as rich. I make a fortune as a bodyguard."

She snorted as she began to walk around the destroyed carcass of her room. Was the safe untouched? "Speaking of which, how does a dog groomer from the UK become an agent at what is clearly a high-end security and protection firm?"

"I'm very convincing at interviews."

Pausing beside the torn remains of her laptop bag—cast aside like a used dishcloth—she fixed him in a level stare.

He shrugged. "I did a hundred pushups?"

"James."

He pulled a breath, eyes closing for a second. "I have a unique set of skills that comes in handy every now and again. Especially to a company dealing in security and protection."

"A unique set of skills?" She narrowed her eyes at him again. "Are you a spook, James? A spy? Or *were* you a spy? MI5? Is that why you took off three years ago without a word?"

"Well, my name *is* James."

Throwing up her hands, she let out a dry bark. "What am I thinking. You're not a spy. I wish you were though. At least that would mean you took off because your life was in danger, or mine, or some flipping shit like that. Not because you didn't love me or want me the way I wanted—"

She slapped her hand to her mouth.

Fuck. She hadn't meant to blurt that out.

"Hope."

"No. Don't 'Hope' me. I just want to get my stuff—whatever stuff I can—and get away."

He didn't move.

She glared at him, waited for him to say something. When he didn't, she stomped over to the cupboard housing her suite's small safe and opened the door.

The safe hung open—and surprisingly, her passport

sat untouched inside. As did the fine gold necklace she couldn't believe she still owned.

Hand shaking, she reached in and withdrew both, tucking her passport into her back pocket before fastening the chain around her neck.

"You didn't throw it away?"

She started at James's low exclamation.

"No," she muttered, turning to face him. "Don't read anything into it." Dropping her gaze, she touched the small genie's lamp pendant once again nestled between her breasts.

"Hope," he murmured.

Why hadn't she been able to throw the damn thing away? She should have ripped it from her neck and tossed it in the Thames the night he'd left.

She hadn't. But she'd tried.

She'd ridden the Tube to the station closest to the river, stomped to the edge, and unclipped the necklace. Balled her fist around it and drew her arm back behind her head, ready to lob it into the fast-moving water.

And then lowered her arm, opened her hand, and fastened the chain back around her neck.

He'd given it to her for her birthday only six months earlier, his smile sheepish as he told her it wasn't expensive, but from his heart.

It was the most precious present she'd ever been given.

She'd walked away from the Thames, muttering about how much she hated him all the way home on the Tube. Took it off her neck and flung it in the top drawer of her bedside table.

Took it back out and returned it to her neck.

Occasionally she took it off and tucked it into her underwear drawer. She just couldn't bring herself to get rid of it, no matter how much it reminded her of James every time she looked at it. In the taxi taking her to Heathrow for her flight to the US, she'd actually stopped the driver a block away from her flat, making him go back so she could get it.

She was an idiot three years ago, she was an idiot twenty-four hours ago, and she was an idiot now for being worried whoever had trashed her room had taken it.

During the drive to the hotel, neither had raised the issue again. The issue of what he'd done three years ago. She'd opened her mouth to do just that the second he put the Jeep Grand Cherokee into gear and drove away from Guarded Souls, but her phone had bleeped with an incoming news alert from her BBC app, about the Prime Minister. She'd read the alert, telling herself it was important, even as she accepted she was avoiding the confrontation.

Schrodinger's Conversation. That's what it was. If she didn't have the conversation with him, she wouldn't find out the real reason he'd taken off and left her.

Fifteen minutes of staring blankly at her phone's screen made her realize how stupid she was being. How gutless. She'd raised her glare to him and—as if aware of her intention—he'd flicked her one of his sheepish smiles.

No. It was a conversation she wasn't ready for, no matter how much she thought she was. So, she'd snapped her mouth shut. She'd spent the rest of the trip pretending to check her email on her phone, scowl firmly in place, ignoring him.

For his part, James had let out a hitching sigh, turned on the music, complained under his breath when it wasn't what he wanted to listen to, and then settled back with a smile when the music suddenly changed to David Bowie singing "Ashes to Ashes".

She'd continued to glare at her phone even as she'd fought the urge to chuckle. David Bowie. James's musical weakness. He used to say David Bowie was the one true musical genius in a world of posers and frauds. Of course finding Bowie on the radio would have sent him into his own world.

Which made the trip here...easier. Brought back bitter-sweet memories of long nights making love to each other in their flat as Bowie played in the background.

Although, now she thought about it, the entire trip had *just* been Bowie from that point. And when had he changed the radio station? She hadn't seen his hand move from the steering wheel.

"Damn you, Hastin," she whispered, lifting her gaze back up to his. "Do you have any idea how much you hurt me? Do you?"

"Yes." His Adam's apple bobbed in his throat. "And if I could take away your pain..."

"I wish I could just forget all about you, James."

His eyes closed at her words. Grief etched his face, as if he were struck by an invisible blow. "Please don't say that."

She'd never heard him sound so wretched.

"*Why* did you leave, James?"

"I..." A wry laugh tore from him as he dragged a hand through his messy hair. "I *wish* I could tell you."

"Did I scare you off?" God. For three years, she'd promised herself if she ever saw him again, she'd never ask him that question. "Did you stop finding me attractive?"

Pain transformed his features, and he closed his eyes. "Tahlee, the only living soul I've ever been attracted to is you. The only person I've ever wanted to be with is you. If nothing else, believe me on—"

She destroyed the small space between them, fisted her hands in his hair and pulled his mouth to hers.

Poured three years of longing and anguish and anger and hunger into the kiss.

And he kissed her back.

With a tormented groan, he kissed her back.

It was like coming home.

His lips moved over hers the way they used to, as if their very lives depended on the passion of the kiss. Life rushed through her. Reason for breath. It had always been this way with James. From their very first kiss. Exhilaration, lust, joy, and comfort beyond comprehension.

She'd instigated that kiss as well...the very first...just as she had this one. Stolen it when they'd been playing darts in a pub in Wimbledon South.

He'd been about to throw the final dart of the game, the one that would—unless he totally fluffed it—leave him the victor.

She'd kissed him to distract him. To stop him from winning.

A few moments later, they'd been asked to leave the pub.

"You can't snog like *that* in public," the barman had complained when they'd come up for air at his shout. "Get a room."

That's exactly what they'd done.

She still didn't remember how they'd made it back to her flat so quickly, but they had, and what they'd started in the pub had finished on her living room floor, their naked bodies sweaty and sticky and joined in the most carnal, natural way.

She'd never forgotten that kiss.

It had been the catalyst for their life together.

This kiss, however...

Tightening her fists in his hair, she rolled her hips, pressing her lower body closer to his. Needing to feel what she hadn't for so long—him. His desire for her. His need.

God, she'd missed it. Craved it.

His hands smoothed up her back as he deepened the kiss, took control of its ferocity.

His tongue mated with hers, demanding and giving back in equal measure. Heat flushed through her, pooling low in the pit of her belly.

She moaned, squeezing her thighs together as the parts of her body she'd thought retired tingled into hot, impatient life.

Raking her hands over his shoulders, she fumbled at the buttons of his shirt. She wanted more.

She wanted the heat of his hard chest beneath her palms again. She wanted the smooth kiss of his six-pack against her fingertips again.

She wanted the broad breadth of his back under her nails as she scored his flesh and branded him as hers once—

No.

Tearing her lips from his, she staggered back a step.

What the flipping hell was she doing?

"I can't believe I did that." She pressed her hand to her mouth, the moisture lingering on her lips from the kiss a mocking blow. "I can't..."

Shaking her head, she turned and strode for the door.

"Hope."

His voice—thick with confusion and shock—flayed at her.

Pivoting on her heel, she stomped back into the bowels of her suite, snatched her laptop bag from the floor, and stormed back to the door.

"Hope."

"No," she threw over her shoulder. "No, we're not talking about this. We're ignoring the fact that *this* ever happened."

Three years.

Three years of getting over the bastard, telling herself it was her own stupid fault for trusting someone.

Trust was for the weak. The foolish.

Trust had allowed her big sister to accept a lift home from school one day with an older boy, instead of catching the DL with Tahlee like she always did. Trust had allowed Tahlee to sit at home, eight years old, waiting for Diahne to arrive, watching television, hungry but knowing she wasn't allowed to eat anything when she was alone.

Trust had allowed Tahlee to tell her mum and dad, at six o'clock that night when they'd gotten home from work, that Diahne would be home soon. She *would*. Diahne had *promised* it was only going to be a quick ride in a car with the boy, and she'd been home soon.

But trust had mocked Tahlee back then. Destroyed her.

Just as it had three years ago.

The difference between Diahne and James, though, was she now knew James was at least alive.

You already knew he was. For three years, you knew. Even if you cursed his name over and over and wished he was dead, you knew he was alive. Every time you looked at the necklace, you knew. You felt it in your soul. As if you were still connected to the bastard, despite him running off.

"Can we just get to the safe house please," she ground out.

"I have to—"

She spun around. "Have to what, James? Make it all better?" Had she ever been so angry?

Yes. Three times. Once at him for leaving, once at yourself for trusting him in the first place. And once at Diahne for letting herself be—

She shook her head. "You lost that right three years ago."

Something dark shimmered in his eyes, and he let out a choppy breath. "I have to do my job, Hope. So to protect you, I need to know who's coming after you."

She swallowed. The soft dejection in his voice smacked her in the chest. Which was ridiculous, given what he'd done to her all those years ago.

"Give me ten minutes," he said. "Five, even. I just want to prowl around a bit to see if I can get any...clues."

Why did it sound like he'd wanted to say something else?

"What's happened to you?" She frowned. "The James standing here now is so different from the James I knew."

A wry laugh fell from him, and he rubbed at the back of his neck before scruffing his hair with both hands, head ducked, that familiar sheepish smile on his face. "Ah, Hope, I wish—" He snorted, rolling his eyes. "I wish you could know how wrong you are."

And with that, he turned and began inspecting the room.

Tahlee narrowed her eyes. What *was* going on here?

Doesn't matter. You didn't come to LA to find a lost love.

Ha. Her journalism professor would slaughter her for such a cliched phrasing. And follow up the slaughter with a dressing-down for getting sidetracked. She was here to expose Minister Simmons's corruption, not uncover what-ever the deal was with James Hastin.

Hell may hath no fury like a woman scorned, but this woman had to keep her focus on the matter at hand.

Despite the little side-trip into possible US political insanity, threats to her life, and a resurrected threat to her heart.

Ah, flipping hell, she needed—

To kiss James again?

"Flipping hell," she muttered, slinging her empty, torn laptop bag onto her shoulder and dumping herself in the nearest chair.

Resting her chin on her fist, she tracked James's move-ment around her suite.

What exactly was he looking for? And how the hell did he think he was going to find whatever it was merely by hovering a palm over things like he was?

And what was he murmuring under his breath?

It didn't sound like English. Nor like any language she'd heard before, and when you were an investigative journalist, you'd pretty much heard every language on the planet.

His background had always intrigued her. He'd passed it off one night, as they lay in bed together watching the latest Doctor Who episode, as being a mixed bag of ancestral heritage. At times, she'd swear his racial background was Middle Eastern, despite the green eyes and light brown hair. Other times, it was as if someone had written a checklist of what made the perfect hot British man, and James was the result. Occa-sionally, she'd detect a slight New Zealand accent, which always made her smile, and from time to time, she'd even get a vibe from him that she could never define...but it somehow made her feel more content and safer than she could fathom.

He'd always been a bit of an enigma, but truthfully, that had been a part of his appeal. That, and the fact she'd felt like she knew him, deep in her heart, from the second she first saw him.

Stop it. You're romanticizing him. Don't do that.

Balling her fist tighter under her chin, she glared at him. "Are you actually going to pick anything up, or are you just trying to look like you know what you're doing?"

He tossed a grin over his shoulder. "I could be wrong, but I'm getting a strong sense of sarcasm in this room right now."

She grunted. Damn him, why did he have such a knack for making her want to smile?

"Is this how you used to groom your dog clients, as well? Wave your hand over their backs, and then use that charm of yours to convince the owners they were shampooed and brushed and clipped?"

"That's exactly how." He moved to the abstract painting that had been hanging above the bed when she'd first checked in. Now it was on the floor near the room's window, broken and sorry. It was too easy to imagine the person responsible for her extreme room redecoration stomping their foot through the generic artwork in frustration when they couldn't find what they were looking for— most likely her.

You should be scared.

She should. Given the state of the room, the destruction in it.

But she wasn't.

And you know why, even if it pisses you off.

She glared again at James, turning up her exasperation

to one hundred. "Is there any chance of you actually doing something anytime soon?"

He dropped into a crouch beside the painting, feathering his fingers over its splintered frame. "Hope, there are two things I want to do right now," he said without looking at her. "One, get anything—no matter how small or insignificant—from this room about the threat to you. And two, kiss you until we're both incapable of standing. The odds are, you're not going to let me do one of them, so I'm going to focus on the other."

She swallowed. "You're a pain in the arse."

"Yep."

He straightened from the broken painting and crossed to the bed, surveying the mess of her upended suitcase strewn all over and around it.

"Did they take any of your clothes?" he asked over his shoulder, focus still on the bed.

"I don't know." She pushed herself from the chair, hitched her laptop bag higher onto her shoulder and crossed to where he stood. "At least they didn't take my favorite bra."

"I remember that bra." He chuckled. "Was partial to it myself."

She laughed, even as she tried to bite it back. "I think I still have the photos of you strutting around our bedroom in it."

He lifted a curious eyebrow at her. "With the matching thong?"

"With the matching thong."

She shouldn't be doing this. She hated him now. Was furious with him. And yet, being with him was like slipping back into the warmth of everything she knew was right and wonderful and comfortable.

His lips curled as he returned his attention to the bed. "Can't see the thong. Did they take it?"

A tight pang stabbed at her chest. Should she tell him she was wearing it now? Or would that throw the whole conversation well and truly over a line it was already teetering on?

Pulse pounding, she opened her mouth.

And gasped when he suddenly spun to face her, stare locked on her laptop bag.

"What—"

"Can I have that?" he almost growled, hooking his fingers around the strap near her breast and sliding it off her shoulder.

She blinked, an icy prickle crawling over her scalp as he grabbed the bag with both hands, knuckles white, and closed his eyes.

What the...

"Shite," he muttered. "This can't be."

He lifted the bag closer to his face, tilting his head to the side, as if listening to it.

Tahlee's stomach clenched. "Are you okay? Or are you having a stroke or something?"

"Shhh." His closed eyes scrunched tighter. A stillness fell over him, except for an almost imperceptible shake of his head. "This can't..." he whispered.

"What can't? James?" She thumped his shoulder with a loose fist. "You're freaking me out a bit."

His eyes snapped open—and she gasped again, staggering back a step.

What the fuck? White...?

Oh God, his eyes are glowing are white! Why are his eyes glowing—

He blinked, his eyes green once more, a choppy laugh falling from his lips.

Tahlee blanched.

Once more? Don't you mean green like they always were? How the flip would they be anything but green?

"Sorry." He ducked his head, handing back her laptop bag. "It's all good. Nothing to freak out about. Bad joke on my behalf. Thought I'd lighten the mood."

"Lighten the..." She gaped at him.

Green eyes regarded her. Green. Not white. Not glowing and iridescent and...and...

Inhuman.

Green.

You're losing your mind, Tahlee.

He tossed one of his sheepish grins at her, and then motioned toward the room's open door. "I've got what I need from here. Ready to go?"

3

Shite.

Shite shite shite.

Shite.

Gripping the Jeep's steering wheel, James stared at the dark road. Kept his expression loose, relaxed, even as his mind raced.

It was impossible. What he'd sensed from Tahlee's laptop bag could not be right.

It couldn't.

The dark magic involved to resurrect...

He swiped at his mouth and cast Tahlee—sound asleep—a frown.

Did she have any inkling, maybe on a subconscious level, what she'd somehow been thrust into?

No, that couldn't be possible, either. That wasn't how it worked.

But still, what are the odds?

Fuck the odds. How was the planet not broken?

Maybe he was wrong. He needed to talk to someone

who could either clarify the impossible, or laugh at him and give him grief for being so wrong.

Shite, he hoped he was wrong.

In the passenger seat, Tahlee snored softly.

He'd missed the very human noise. Missed it more than he could comprehend, in fact. When she'd first started snoring—twenty minutes into the drive to the Guarded Souls safe house high in the Topanga Canyon hills—he'd forgotten the nightmare scenario trying to take up residence in his head and had, for a few wonderful moments, savored the sounds of Tahlee resting peacefully.

Sounds he'd never forget, no matter how many centuries unfurled around him.

Sounds he still ached for every time he allowed himself the luxury of repose. Falling asleep—such a human thing to do—to the soft sound of Tahlee's deep breathing had been one of his favorite things. Ever. In all his eons of existence, those delicate little buzzing sounds had filled him with serenity unlike any other.

He'd grinned when she'd first started snoring from the passenger seat, allowing himself to be lost to a fantasy so long denied him.

Until the memory of what he'd sensed from her laptop bag interfered.

The situation Tahlee had somehow landed in had removed the grin from his face straight away.

He'd gripped the steering wheel hard enough to send shards of very human pain through the bones of his hand and up his arms, and kept it that way.

Better to be in constant pain that to forget the reason he couldn't listen to Tahlee sleep every night.

Now, with at least ten miles to go before they reached the safe house—how did humans ever get anything done when so much time was wasted on driving?—he glared at the road.

Taking Tahlee somewhere safe wasn't enough. Not if what he'd sensed was correct.

"Shite," he exhaled, giving her another quick look.

She was so beautiful and fierce and frustrating—and he would destroy the world if something happened to her.

With a cold click of his fingers.

Destroy it, resurrect it, and destroy it again.

That's not what you do, who you are anymore, Barqan.

James sucked in a breath. Barqan. It had been a long time since he'd allowed that name to enter his mind. A lifetime.

Ha. A lifetime? Don't you mean fifteen lifetimes? Or is it more?

Something dark slithered through him. Dark and angry. Something long buried in his soul.

Something awoken by what he'd sensed from Tahlee's laptop bag.

The bones in his knuckles burned as he squeezed the wheel tighter. For the first time in centuries, he wondered if it was time to reach out to his fellow djinn.

His gut clenched at the thought.

Since their creation countless millennia ago, djinn were pack creatures. And yet, as the centuries passed, those who'd acclimatized to life with humans had become more solo in their behavior. And less trusting of their fellow djinn.

There weren't many of his kind existing in the realm of mankind. Not at the moment, at least. And only one of them foolish enough to get himself stranded here. Those who could still traverse back and forth to the djinn home realm sniggered at the one stuck in the home world.

James hated sniggering.

As it turned out, those who sniggered learned very quickly not to be anywhere near James.

Fighting amongst djinn didn't happen often, but when it did...well, he'd never started a fight, but he would *always* be the one to finish it.

Which meant any help he asked for from his fellow djinn would be refused. Or more likely ignored.

"Shite."

So who did he ask?

Feathers was a possibility, but as far as James knew, the angel couldn't tap into forces from realms different to his own or that of mankind. Need to know anything about human souls? Nathanial had it covered. Need to know when a water sprite was planning to cause a drowning? The angel could likely shrug those magnificent wings of his and find the answer.

The temporal plane and the ethereal plane were no match for Nathanial, but the djinn realm? Now, that was a different story.

Nim? The wiccan *might* be able to tap into the djinn realm. She'd have no luck navigating it though, which meant seeking another djinn to help her—which, again, would be futile.

She might, however, be able to detect what he'd sensed from Tahlee's bag. It was intrinsically entwined with dark magic, after all. The darkest, in fact.

Too dark for Nim? Will it put her existence at risk?

Could he do that? Risk Nim for Tahlee?

The answer to that clenched his heart.

For Tahlee, he'd—

"We there yet?"

He blinked at Tahlee's mumbled question, forced a

loose grin to his face and let out a low chuckle. "I forgot how much you snore."

"I do *not* snore." She shifted in the seat, dragging her hands through the thick curtain of her hair, before stretching like a cat and yawning like a hippo.

Sucking in a long breath, he fixed his focus on the dark road.

You are in so much trouble, James.

"We're about fifteen minutes away. Maybe." He forced out an unperturbed laugh. "The GPS thingy stopped talking to me a while ago. But I remember where we are now. It looks familiar."

The "GPS thingy" would never be able to navigate directly to the Guarded Souls safe house, given the different levels of magical wards and security spells cast upon it. When it came to keeping the place off anyone's radar—human and nonhuman alike—Kade didn't mess around.

James had never driven here before, but the tingling in his djinn soul told him exactly where they were and where to go.

Want something? Think about it, contemplate it, and either get it or get *to* it. That was the djinn way.

Tempering that power so he could maintain the illusion of being human was easy. Frustrating to be sure, but easy.

What he should have done was click his fingers and transport them to the safe house the moment Tahlee fell asleep. Of course, Tahlee being Tahlee, she would have immediately noticed the time leap and demanded answers.

And while he loved when she demanded answers about corrupt CEOs and public servants and medical practitioners for the articles she wrote, demanding answers about anything to do with *him*...

Yeah, well, he was already in danger of her noticing his weird behavior since their unexpected reunion, so driving all the way to the safe house it was.

"So when we get there," she said, narrowing her eyes at the dark bushes and trees outside the car, "you're going, right?"

"What?" He raised his eyebrows.

"I'll be safe there." she said. "Safe. House. You don't need to hang around. I can take care of myself. And I'm pretty certain you don't want to be forced to babysit me. Given our...history."

"You heard Kade. I'll be hanging around until the threat to you is neutralized."

Or, if it's who I think it is, annihilated. Decimated. For starters.

Silence answered him.

He risked a quick glance at her.

She frowned at him, bottom lip caught between her teeth. "In that case, we've got two obvious options," she finally said. "We can talk it out, finally lance the festering boil that was once our happy relationship before you fucked it up. Or we can pretend it never happened—*we* never happened—and the only relationship you and I have is that of protector and reluctant protected."

"Hm, let me guess which one you want to pick."

"Schrodinger's Conversation be damned!" she burst out. She spun to face him, grabbing at the dashboard with one hand and stabbing the index finger of the other into his biceps. "I'm going to pick the first flipping one. And seeing as you're instructed by your boss to constantly look after me, anytime you think of trying to dodge the conversation by walking away from me, I'm going to duct tape you to a chair. And don't even *think* of going to the toilet without me tagging along. Oh no. Once bitten, a million times shy when it comes to you ever going to the toilet mid-conversation again. If we're stuck together in a flipping safe house, then I'm making the most of it. I'm not letting you out of my sight until I've got—"

"We're here," James stated, pulling to a halt at the front of the safe house.

Tahlee snapped her mouth shut, stare locked on the dark building nestled amongst dense bushes and towering trees. "Well," she said, frowning. "It's not exactly how I pictured it."

"Kade has..." He scratched at the scruff on his jaw. "How shall I put this? Farking expensive tastes."

Kade had more money than he knew what to do with. Came with being a vampire older than dirt with a good head for business and stocks and investments. Plus, it helped that he'd spent centuries cultivating relationships that ultimately paid out. Christen and Daku had started a pool on how many famous figures from history Kade had known. Of course, the wight and the ancient dreamwalker had differing opinions on what kinds of relationships he'd had with said famous figures, one opinion being far more explicit than the other.

Christen—being a Norse nature spirit—tended to be more wholesome in his ideas. Dak, well—the dreamwalker veered more toward the debauched. He did, after all, spend an inordinate number of hours submerged in the dreams of others.

"This is really the safe house?" Tahlee let out a low whistle. "The bodyguard business obviously pays well."

James laugh. "You have no idea."

The money some Guarded Souls clients threw at Kade made James wince, which was saying something, given all he had to do was click his fingers and he'd drown in money.

Money, however, had never been alluring to him. Why would it? When he wanted something, he just thought of the item and he got it. For as long as he wanted it.

Yeah. Except for one thing.

The only *true* desire he had, the one thing he wanted, was denied him.

Forever.

Thanks to the farking iniquitous, heinous—

Clearing his throat, James opened the Jeep's driver-side door and climbed out.

He needed clarification. Before he unraveled and did something foolish.

And allowing yourself to be in Tahlee's company around the clock isn't?

Closing his door, he moved to the passenger side. Fast.

Too fast.

Damn it, he needed to control himself.

How many years had he lived with her? And not once had he ever come close to revealing what he truly was.

Well, if he didn't count the time on the dance floor in the pub in Covent Gardens.

Still, even that incident paled next to one second being on the driver's side of the Jeep, and the next, being on the passenger's side, opening the door for Tahlee.

Who frowned at him now.

Confusion warred with surprise in her eyes. "Wow. That was...quick. Really quick."

He dropped her a wink and dipped a little at the waist.

"Expect only the best from your Guarded Soul personal bodyguard, Hope. That's the company motto."

She rolled her eyes.

"Actually," he tapped a finger to his lips, "I think the company motto is 'Back off, bad guys.'"

Gripping the strap of her laptop bag, she climbed out of the Jeep. "One of these days you're going to take something seriously, James Hastin, and I wish like flipping hell I'll be there to see it."

He let out a silent sigh. If only she knew she already had.

"C'mon," he said, closing the passenger door, and waving a hand toward the dark safe house. "I'll make you a cup of tea."

"Good. We can continue our conversation over a cuppa."

Shite. He should have known he hadn't been that lucky.

Wishes for *other* people, he could grant. Wishing Tahlee would make this easy? That was beyond even his phenomenal cosmic powers. He was good, but not *that* good. He couldn't perform the impossible, no matter how much he wanted to.

"Yay," he said.

Tahlee chuckled. "And you thought you'd distracted me."

He couldn't help but smile. "I was hoping."

"You know what they say, James. If wishes were horses."

"You want a horse?" If he clicked his fingers right now, if he made a horse—a Clydesdale? Or an Arabian?—instantly appear in front of the safe house, maybe then she'd stop asking why he'd taken off three years ago.

Yeah, and that's *the solution to the problem.*

"I want answers." She nudged his shoulder with her fist, her smile part playful, part cutting, before she began walking toward the safe house. "And then maybe after that you can buy me a horse."

James rubbed at the back of his neck. This was not going to be easy.

"I'm assuming you can get in?" Tahlee called to him from the front door.

"Yeah," he called back, striding toward her. "The lock is a proximity system. It'll open to my phone."

The system had nothing to do with such a thing, but it was an easier explanation than the truth. At least the truth for James.

Climbing the low stairs leading up to the front door, he clicked his right fingers, low, beside his thigh. The door unlocked, swung open a little, and all the lights in the house turned on.

"Impressive." Tahlee folded her arms beneath her breasts and leaned her hip against the doorframe. "If a tad ostentatious."

James chuckled. If Kade had been there, he would be grumbling under his breath about bastard djinn and their complete disrespect for protocol.

Who needed a key and a code when you had a thumb and a middle finger?

He grinned. "Why, yes, I am. Thank you."

Rolling her eyes, Tahlee stepped over the threshold and into the safe house. "Let's get on with it then."

James swallowed, watching her walk. Hips swaying with a natural grace, dark hair tumbling down her back in a thick, wavy curtain, long legs carrying her farther away from him with confident strides.

It was too easy to remember what those legs felt like wrapped around his hips. Too easy to remember the feel of her hair brushing his face as she straddled his hips, smiling down at him just before kissing him, her hands pinning his wrists to the mattress beside his head, her low, throaty laugh vibrating through both their bodies.

"Shite," he ground out, rubbing at the back of his neck before clawing his fingers over his scalp.

Of course, he *could* just tell Kade to stick this job. He didn't need to work. None of the nonhumans did, really. But he liked hanging with the Guarded Souls team. He liked the rush he got from keeping defenseless humans safe—even the annoying wealthy ones. It didn't come close to the rush of granting wishes, but it sometimes felt more real.

He didn't need to work, and he didn't—strictly speaking—need to do what Kade instructed him to do. Stay with Tahlee.

But he wouldn't ignore her.

He never could.

Which damned him to an existence of torture and torment. Exactly what the farking sorcerer had intended.

Perhaps you're finally going to get the chance to fix it?

Raking his fingers over his scalp again, he closed the door behind him, locked it—in both the traditional and magical senses—and followed Tahlee into the house.

He couldn't allow himself the luxury of believing such a thing. If what he'd sensed from her laptop bag *was* accurate, there was no silver lining in the nightmare.

If the sorcerer who'd summoned him to mankind's realm over fourteen hundred years ago was alive once again, and Tahlee had inadvertently caught the malevolent bastard's attention, everything he knew was threatened.

Including himself.

You need to be sure.

"I'm just going to take a quick look around," he called, striding away from Tahlee, who was making her way to the living room. "Make yourself at home."

"Ha," she called back. "So you want me to whip off my bra, strip down to my undies and T-shirt, and watch reruns of *Coronation Street*?"

An image of Tahlee doing just that in their old flat back in Wimbledon filled James's head, and he bit back a groan. She'd come home from work, pull her bra off from beneath her shirt, toss it at him, strip off whatever she was wearing on the bottom half of her body, drop onto his lap, and kiss him senseless before they'd settle in for the night, relaxing, watching TV, making love...

Shite, he missed that life.

Stop it.

"Dare you, Hope," he called back. The trouble was, with a response like that, Tahlee was the kind of person to do it. Just to get under his skin. She had the moral upper hand right now, and would play dirty to keep it.

Yeah, he truly missed his life with her.

Stop. It.

He hurried toward the back of the house, into a room set up like a private cinema, complete with luxurious leather reclining armchairs, a massive screen and a fully stocked bar in the corner.

Kade had too much money. Way too much money.

Swinging the door shut behind him, he stopped in the middle of the space between the chairs and the screen and let out a slow breath.

He needed to do something. Quickly.

Did he risk narrowing his thoughts onto the presence

he'd sensed on Tahlee's laptop bag? If he did, and the impossible was, in fact, possible, he risked either going straight to the bastard sorcerer or bringing the bastard sorcerer to him.

Both could possibly put Tahlee at risk.

And what about yourself? What would Syrin do if he came face to face with you after all these centuries?

He needed help.

Okay, he'd ask Nim. If nothing else, the wiccan would be able to clarify if a powerful sorcerer walked the earth. Again. When he should be dead. Deader than dead. *Un*made.

With another deep breath, James concentrated on Nim. Pictured the petite woman with her purple buzz-cut pixie hair, multiple piercings up the length of her right ear, her intricate tattoo of a phoenix rising up her left thigh, and her striking blue eyes.

Focused on her existence.

And clicked his fingers.

Nothing.

"What the..." he muttered, frowning.

All he had to do to project an echo of himself to someone was think about them, and voila, he was there. Well...half there, half where he was.

It was instant and accurate.

Normally.

"Where the hell are you, Nim?"

He intensified the image of her in his mind.

Nothing. It was as if she didn't exist.

She did, of course. He'd watched her eat a bowl of noodles less than twenty-four hours ago. Nim was ferocious and snarky and full of bite and sunshine. She was one of his favorite humans, even if she did have a thing for turning his tea to coffee whenever he beat her in the weekly office betting pool on how many times Christen would swear at the staffroom microwave.

"Alright, Nimeu," he muttered, closing his eyes as he rolled his head and shook out his shoulders. "Show yourself."

Nope. Nothing.

"Well, this is farking inconvenient." Shaking his head, he drew a slow breath, formed an image of Kitt in his head, and clicked his fingers.

And projected his image into Kitt's kitchen.

The dawn sun streamed through the large window running the length of the room, casting the wolf shifter—wearing only sweatpants, and pouring himself a coffee—in a golden hue.

"Morning, Rover," James said, throwing Kitt a smile. "Wanna play fetch?"

"Shit!" Kitt dropped his coffee, caught the mug by its handle just before it hit the floor, and then glared at James. "Hastin, you smoky son of a..." Straightening, he flicked spilled coffee from his hand, swiped it dry on his sweatpants, and glared harder at James. "What the hell are you doing in my kitchen?"

"I need to talk to Nim, but I can't locate her."

"She's on assignment." Kitt poured more coffee into his still-dripping mug, rested his butt against the kitchen counter, and crossed his ankles. "Unreachable. Even to you."

James let out a ragged sigh. "Kade's orders?"

"Kade's orders." Kitt took a sip before smacking his lips together in melodramatic appreciation. "He suspected you'd try to shirk your duties looking after Ms. Hope. Or ask someone to come lend a hand. Or to run interference."

"Sneaky bastard."

Kitt snorted. "I was there when you first laid eyes on her in Kade's office, Jimmy Boy. I've never seen a man want to both run in the opposite direction quick smart *and* throw himself at a woman there and then. It was very entertaining."

"I'm glad my conundrum amuses you, Rover." James raked a hand through his hair. "But I've got a legit situation, and I need help."

Kitt's eyebrows lifted. "Sorry, did the genie just admit to needing help?"

"The genie did. The genie is, possibly, in a shite-load of trouble."

Kitt frowned. "Shit, you're not kidding, are you?"

James sighed. "I wish I was, for once."

"What's going on? What can I do to help?"

James studied Kitt. He'd never told *anyone* why he was trapped in the human realm. No one knew, not even Kade or Feathers—and the vamp and the angel had unique ways of knowing almost everything.

"James." Kitt placed his coffee mug on the counter, crossed his arms over his chest, and met his wary stare. "Let me fucking help you. What's going on?"

Swallowing, James clawed at his scalp again. "Shite."

"Talk to me, James." Worry etched Kitt's face. "Please."

Letting out a raw breath, James dipped his head in a nod. "Okay. So this is it—fourteen-hundred years ago, I was summoned to mankind's realm by a sorcerer in what's now known as Wiltshire."

"Wiltshire? In the UK?"

"Yeah, where Stonehenge is." James snorted. "It looked very different back then, trust me. He summoned me in a ritual involving a sacrificial goat and some other messed-up shit—which is the traditional way a djinn is brought to this realm—and requested I stop his village from dying of a sickness *he* himself inadvertently created. I did. Took me a while, cost him a lot in wishes, but I did. And I fell in love with his daughter at the same time."

"Whoa."

"Whoa. Yeah, that's about right. I didn't mean to, but Rose... She was so kind, so funny, so gentle and fierce and...and..." Her smile filled his head. His heart beat faster. For a split second, Kitt's kitchen blurred, grew faint, fainter, replaced with a sweeping grassy field and thatch-roofed huts, and the silhouette of a woman watching the morning sun peek over the distant horizon.

Rose...

"Rose," he whispered.

"What happened to her?"

Kitt's low voice rumbled through the soft *cree* of crickets, and James blinked, the wolf-shifter's kitchen surrounding him once more.

Rose...

Heart tearing, he let out a shaky breath. "When Syrin learned his daughter was in love with me as well, he cast a spell to erase my existence. But it backfired...and killed Rose instead."

"Shit."

"And in doing so—"

"What the hell?" Tahlee's cry filled the room. "*James?*"

Shite!

He spun around, stare clashing with hers.

"R—Tahlee? Shite, I didn't lock the door? I thought I'd... You weren't meant to see—"

"Crap," Kitt growled.

Tahlee staggered back a step, eyes enormous. "Why...

What? Oh my God, James, I can see *through* you! *Why can I see through you?* Oh my God, what the *fuck* is going on?"

SOMETHING WASN'T RIGHT.

Philips ran his index finger through the bowl, forming a line in the warm red liquid pooling shallowly at the bottom.

No. Not right at all.

The blood slicked the ceramic surface, interrupted by the path made by his finger, retreating from his flesh.

He narrowed his eyes, his heart thumping. This was not good.

Something was wrong.

The spell was a simple one, designed to locate a missing person. Sure, it required blood, but blood magic rarely caused him grief.

Except this time...

Lifting his arm above the bowl, he fisted his hand and, with his other index finger, stretched the cut he'd made in his wrist, opening it wider.

He murmured the incantation again, voice low, stare locked on the fresh blood dripping from the raw wound as he concentrated his thoughts on the woman from the Getty.

As he chanted the incantation under his breath, the ancient words thrumming through his body, he repeated her name in his head.

Tahlee Hope.

His blood bubbled and sizzled as it hit the base of the bowl, agitated.

He frowned, even as he narrowed his focus harder on

the elusive bitch. Incantation complete—for the second time—he lowered his hand and traced his finger through the new blood mingling with the old.

Again, the warm liquid parted with his finger's path.

"Fuck."

Wherever Tahlee Hope was, she was protected by some serious magic.

"*Fuck*!" he shouted, flinging the bowl off the table and across the room with a swipe of his hand. Blood splashed onto his face and, wincing, he smeared it over his lips and neck.

This was his third attempt to locate her since she'd disappeared from the West LA Community Police Station.

The first attempt—using the blood of the imbecilic grunt who'd failed to grab her when she'd first left the cops—had failed spectacularly. It had been a long time since Philips saw a corpse turn inside out during a spell. The deceased grunt had done just that, spraying guts and blood and ichor around Philips's private office halfway through what should have been a simple invocation.

He should have known finding her wasn't going to be a simple task the second he'd learned her existence was somehow concealed.

The question was, by whom?

Whatever the tall man in the dark suit had done to the detective who'd taken her statement, the cop was incapable of revealing his name or who he worked for.

The only thing Philips could get out of him was the woman's name: Tahlee Hope. And even *that* had been like pulling teeth from a live bull.

Philips, however, had pulled many teeth from living beings, both literally and metaphorically. Extracting the name of the woman who'd overheard his conversation in the men's toilet had raised a sweat, but he'd finally gotten it.

The cop might not remember the name of his friends or family for a while—or indeed, his own name—but that was no matter. No one could link Philips to him. The cop had simply decided to go for coffee at two in the morning and had come back...damaged.

Glaring at the blood-spattered table, Philips straightened to his feet and crossed his office to the bar.

It should have been easier than this. Searching her hotel room had revealed nothing. Once he had the woman's name, he should have been able to locate her.

"So who the fuck is hiding her?"

He didn't know.

In all his years, this was the first time he'd encountered other magic he couldn't defeat.

Throughout his childhood and teenage years, he'd encountered no magic at all. Certainly those sluts during his senior year in high school, the ones who'd bragged about being witches, hadn't actually been practitioners.

He'd shown them what it meant to truly wield magic, one night when he'd lured them to his parents' home.

They'd arrived, dressed in cliched skanky Goth attire, eyeliner so dark it was a wonder their lids hadn't stuck together when they blinked, weighed down by chains and studs and their own delusions that they were powerful witches. And they'd laughed at him when he'd said he was a wizard.

They'd quickly stopped laughing—and started screaming and groveling, submitting to everything he wanted to do to them. They'd never said a word about it to anyone after he was finished.

He'd shown them.

Of course, he'd since learned he *wasn't* a wizard. He hadn't learned anything about the craft; it had been born to him. He was a sorcerer. Born with powers beyond his understanding as a child, beyond his imagination as an adult.

Powers that allowed him to punish and destroy and torture those he deemed against him. Powers that allowed him to massage the lives of those beneficial to him.

Powers that allowed him to shape, manipulate, control and enslave.

Powers that allowed him to get everything he wanted.

Except it seemed those powers couldn't fucking find Tahlee fucking Hope's location, no matter how much he wanted it.

Snatching up the bottle of whiskey, he splashed some into a glass.

Where the fuck was she?

He'd had to resort to Google to learn she was a journalist from the UK. The moment he'd read that word, *journalist*, his skin had crawled.

A scourge, a muckraker. What the fuck had she been doing in the men's toilet at the Getty?

It was only an itch in his gut that had made him look back at the door in time to see someone leave the restroom. A short female in jeans.

He'd been waylaid by Rourke before he could follow her out of the museum, and he'd quickly thrown a hooking spell onto her soul. The spell faded within the hour, but it was long enough for him to learn she'd left the museum and headed straight for the West LA Community Police Station.

And then his incompetent grunt had lost her completely, and he'd had to step in himself. He didn't mind getting his hands dirty, but he already had one bitch to deal with, and the last thing he needed was a journalist hearing something she shouldn't.

Fuck.

Was she investigating Rourke? He'd spent many years manipulating Maximillian Rourke's life, massaging his path. Had dedicated untold hours making sure the businessman ended up exactly where Philips wanted him to end up—and he was *not* going to allow all that time and energy to be undone by a nosy limey bitch.

Was she here in the US because of Rourke? Or for other reasons? Were those other reasons why he couldn't locate her now?

Was something happening he hadn't foreseen? Did he have a rival? Was someone else pulling strings he'd thought only *he* controlled?

"Fuck!" The glass of whisky shattered as he threw it against the wall. He did not like this. *He* controlled everything he wanted, not some unseen...what? Mage? Witch? Wizard?

Sorcerer?

Surely not. He would have detected someone of that status, that power.

Are you sure? You've killed more than one over the years. Perhaps this one is hiding?

"*Fuck!*" He smashed his fists onto the bar.

Three attempts at locating Tahlee Hope. Three failures. He'd never failed to locate someone using his own blood. Never.

Which meant whoever was protecting her was powerful. Powerful enough to suppress their identity from the detective's memory; powerful enough to conceal Tahlee Hope's presence from him.

Powerful magic.

When he found the practitioner, he would slit their throat, drain them of their blood, and absorb their magic and life force, as he had every practitioner of magic he'd ever encountered.

Once that was done, he'd strip *everything* from Tahlee Hope's mind. Reduce her to a human vegetable.

And *then*, he'd rip out her tongue and toss her to the sharks.

Whoever was protecting her might be hiding her life force, but when *he* was finished, her life—and the lives of those foolishly protecting her—would be null and void. Erased.

Unmade.

All he had to do was find her.

Drawing a deep breath, he crossed back to his desk, selected one of the numerous burner phones, and called a number plucked from the detective's mind.

"Taylor residence," a timid female voice said through the connection.

"Mrs. Taylor?" He poured a world of compassion and sympathy and kindness into his voice. "This is Doctor... Quincy. I apologize for calling so early but I've just seen the ER reports from your husband's tests."

"Oh my God," Mrs. Taylor blubbered. "I don't understand what's happening to him! Since he was released from the ER, he keeps forgetting things. Is it a stroke?"

Philips ground his teeth and forced out a calming sound. "I think I know what to do. I know it's a rather unusual request, but I'm hoping you can bring him to me? At my private residence? There's something I need to check out."

"Really? You'd...you'd do... Oh, thank you, Doctor!"

More blubbering and tears from the detective's wife. "Thank you! Yes. I'll bring him straight away. Just let me get a pen to write your address. Oh, thank you, thank you."

Philips smiled, swirling his finger through the blood splatters on his desk. "You're more than welcome, Mrs. Taylor. You're more than welcome."

4

She ran.

Bolted through the safe house. Straight for the front door.

James... James had been...

Transparent!

"Tahlee!" he shouted behind her.

...cast a spell to erase my existence...

The words she'd overheard him say in the cinema room screamed through her head.

...killed Rose instead...

Transparent.

Cast a spell.

Killed.

Oh God!

She ran faster—and slammed into a hard, warm body.

"Hope." Strong fingers curled around her upper arms. "Stop."

She screamed. Gibbered up at him. How the fuck had he gotten in front of her?

"Hope." His grip on her arms tightened. "Honey, please."

She smashed her knee into his groin, thrashed out of his hold as he doubled over, shoved him aside, and started running again.

"Stay away from me!" she yelled over her shoulder.

Transparent. He'd been *transparent*. She'd been able to see through him.

See through—

"Hope."

He appeared in front of her again.

She hit the brakes, fell on her arse, scrambled to her feet and ran in the opposite direction.

Oh God, what the flipping hell was going on?

Maybe she was dreaming?

"Tahlee." He materialized out of nowhere, directly in her path.

"Stop that!" she screamed, flailing backward and landing on her arse again.

She half spun, half clambered to her feet and ran for the door once more.

Dream. Gotta be a dream. James can't—

He appeared out of thin air in front of her. "Please, let me—"

She dropped her shoulder, drove it into his side, and continued running. Thank you, five years of private-girls-school rugby.

The front door loomed before her. Teasing her.

So close. Closer.

And then James appeared again. One second not there, the next there.

There.

Stumbling to a halt, head roaring, heart racing, she

bent over and pressed her hands to her knees, staring at him as she sucked in a shaky breath. "I don't... What *are* you?"

He let out an equally shaky laugh, palms facing her. "It's better if you just keep thinking of me as James."

"*What are you?*" she screamed, stamping her foot.

"Hope—"

"No!" She stabbed a finger at him. "You don't get to do that! We lived together. We had sex every night. I fucking fell in *love* with you! You don't get to tell me—after I see you standing there *transparent*—to just think of you as James. What. Are. You?"

Closing his eyes, he dropped his head and rubbed at the back of his neck.

"And don't you *dare* think you can sheepish-grin your way out of this," she snarled. Prickling heat burned away the suffocating ice of her fear. Her blood roared in her ears. "That's not going to work this time."

Or ever again.

"Okay." He lowered his hand and met her stare.

"Good." Sucking in another breath, she crossed her arms over her breasts and narrowed her eyes. "Did I just see what I think I did? Did you just...*do* what I think you did?"

It wasn't possible. Now that fear wasn't turning her into a shrieking idiot, she realized it wasn't possible. She had to be seeing things.

"Or did you drug me on the way here?" She'd researched mind-altering drugs and hallucinogenics for an article a year ago. What some of the shit out there could do to a person's brain...

"What answer do you want, Hope?" He studied her, expression steady. Calm, of all things, given the ridiculous situation. "The truth? Or the one that'll make you feel better?"

A cold finger slid up her spine at his question. It wasn't the response she was expecting.

What is?

Another Schrodinger's Conversation. She was in another flipping Schrodinger's Conversation. Right now. But this one felt more...monumental.

He'd either drugged her, or she was insane.

She fought the urge to hug herself, studying the man she'd once loved. The only man she'd *ever* loved. If he told her he'd drugged her, she could hate him all over again. It would tear her apart, but she'd survive it.

It made sense. It was the only logical explanation.

If he told her she *hadn't* seen through him back in the cinema room, hadn't heard him talking about spells to erase his existence and someone called Rose being killed, she'd have to question her own sanity—and there was no way she was insane.

If he gave her another reason for his transparency...

No. There can't be another reason. This is ridiculous. Get out of here. Now. Just get away. Before he says something you can never unhear.

"I want the truth, James," she said, tilting her chin. She wasn't running away. Screw that. "As I always do. I want the truth. You of all people should know that."

His Adam's apple slid up and down his throat and his eyes fluttered closed.

Christ, why did he have to be so *flipping* gorgeous? Why did her stupid heart have to remember so clearly how incredible it was to be in love with him?

You still are *in love with him. You never stopped. No matter how much you hate him, you still love him.*

"Just tell me the truth, James," she whispered. "Please?"

Opening his eyes, he nodded. "The truth. Okay." He pressed his palms together, gaze holding hers. "Here we go. I'm an ancient, ageless djinn who was summoned to medieval Britain by a sorcerer during the seventh century, and have been trapped here in mankind's realm ever since."

She blinked.

And then burst out laughing.

"Okay, I did *not* see that coming." She staggered back a step, laughter making her wobbly. "A djinn? I'm assuming you mean like a genie, not the drink? As in D-J-I-N-N? Where's your lamp? You'd think after living with you for over a year, I would have noticed the lamp. Can you grant me a wish? Or do I have to rub something first?" She rolled her eyes, the laughter in her lungs turning sharp. "Oh wait, let me guess. You're not *that* kind of genie. Do I have to rub something else? No wonder you were such a fan of hand jobs when we were—"

"Tahlee," he said. "I'm not lying. I've never lied to you."

Her eyebrows shot up so fast her forehead hurt. "Never lied to... Oh my God, are you *kidding*? You just told me you're an ancient genie, but you spent all those years we were living together telling me you were a dog groomer. So which is true, James? Huh? Which one's the lie?"

Was he being serious? Surely not? Did he think she was a gullible moron?

"Neither." He let out a choppy breath and raked a hand through his hair. "I made all the money I earned back then grooming dogs. I enjoyed the work. Dogs are awesome."

"Dogs are..." She shook her head, a dry laugh tearing at her throat. "I thought I was maybe going out of my mind, but clearly *you've* lost it, James."

He studied her. "Maybe."

He was transparent! You saw that! You saw through him. Are you just going to pretend you didn't?

Had she? Had she really?

Yes. She had. And when she'd run from what she'd seen, he'd followed her.

No, he'd repeatedly *materialized* in front of her. She'd seen that. One second he hadn't been in front of her, and then he had. Over and over.

...cast a spell to erase my existence...

His earlier words, spoken to an empty room, whispered through her head again.

She'd gone looking for him, to suggest she make them both a cup of tea before she gave him a good piece of her mind for deserting her three years ago. She'd followed his voice to the back of the large house. He'd been talking to someone, although she'd only heard *him*. She'd reached the barely opened door to a room, her heart pumping faster at the worry, the agitation she'd detected in his voice coming through the crack. James never worried. James was unflappable. Maybe she really was in danger, if he sounded like that?

She'd pressed her hand to the door and gently swung it open, enough for her to walk into the room.

...cast a spell to erase my existence, he'd said, as if involved in a conversation with someone right in front of him, *but it backfired, and killed Rose instead.*

She remembered wondering what he was doing, who he thought he was talking to. Wondering who Rose was.

And that's when she'd noticed he was transparent. That's when she'd noticed, truly realized, she could see right through him.

Staring at him now, she swallowed.

Was it real? Had she really seen through him? Had he really been transparent?

Yes.

Yes, he had.

Her knees gave out.

And before she could blink, he was at her side, like impossibly fast smoke, his hands gently catching her as she crumpled toward the floor.

"I've got you," he murmured, halting her fall.

Head swimming, stomach lurching, she frowned up at him. "I...I..."

Words wouldn't come. Refused to. What words would make any sense?

"I..."

"I know," he said, releasing one of her hands to smooth his arms around her back. "It's not what you were expecting."

She blinked. "You..."

Where were her words? She was normally so good at them. Why weren't they forming on her tongue now?

"G-geen..." She licked lips suddenly drier than dirt. "*Genie*. Like...like Aladdin..."

"Djinn," he murmured, walking them both back toward the living room. "Not quite what Hollywood would have you believe."

She stopped, pulling away from him a little even as she grabbed tight at his hand. "Can you read my mind?"

He chuckled, the sound so like the wry laughs from their past together that, for a moment, she wondered if she really was dreaming. It would make so much more sense. "No. You actually said that aloud."

"Did I?" Her head swam again. Her stomach did the same. "I don't... I don't feel—"

The living room vanished, replaced by a large, spacious bathroom.

She gasped, gaping at the toilet directly in front of her.

"Why...? What...?" She turned to gape at James. "Did *you* bring us here?"

"Yes."

She frowned. "*Why*?"

Confusion etched his face. "You looked like you were about to throw up."

"I *was* about to throw up! I just found out the man I love—*loved*—is a flipping genie!"

"Djinn."

"But *now* I'm just pissed! You...you...*zapped* me through space without asking for permission!" She detangled herself from his gentle hold and smacked the back of her hand into his chest. "Don't you ever do that again!"

"Hey." He took a step back, rubbing his chest. "Don't hurt the bodyguard."

She threw up her hands. "God, I wish you could just be serious for— Shit!" She slapped her hands over her mouth, staring at him.

"What?"

Removing her hand—a little—she frowned again. "I just said *wish*. Does that...?"

He arched an eyebrow, expression stoic. "Yes. You've doomed me to being serious for all time, Tahlee Hope."

Her heart slammed into her throat.

His lips twitched.

She whacked the back of her hand into his chest again. "That is not funny, James Hastin. Not funny!"

A grin played with his lips some more. "It's a little funny."

"No. It isn't."

Screw him. Djinn or not, she didn't have to put up with this.

Spinning on her heel, she stomped out of the bathroom and through the safe house.

It truly was gorgeous. And massive. And decorated with a sense of timeless style she'd never be able to create herself. Her flat back in Wimbledon was an eclectic mix of cluttered chaos and thrift-store bargains, and would have fit entirely in the living room and kitchen of this place.

She loved her flat, though. Every part of it was a story, a diary of her life.

Including all the parts that tell the story of you and James. The parts you couldn't bring yourself to give away.

Stopping at the luxurious leather lounge in the living room, she pressed her palms to her face.

James. James was a genie. A *djinn*. A mythical being. A magical creature. A supernatural...

"Oh boy," she mumbled, knees wobbling again.

She dropped onto the lounge just as James appeared beside her, in that same freaky blur of purple smoke he'd become when she'd collapsed near the front door.

"Hope?"

"I'm okay." She waved her hand above her head as she stared at the floor between her feet. "I mean, I'm not okay, but I'll *be* okay. I think."

The lounge dipped beside her, James's warmth radiating into her side. A hand smoothed over her back, and she closed her eyes. How many nights had he rubbed her back in the same way, after she'd had a shit day at work and had ranted and raved about the corrupt bastards of the world?

So many. Every stroke and caress of his hand had made her feel better back then, melting away her stress and agitation until she'd let out a grateful, appreciative hum and settled into his side, content and comforted.

Sitting upright, she twisted on the cushion and fixed him with a fierce glare. "Did you use your magic genie powers on me when we were together? To make me fall in love with you?"

"No."

"Don't lie to me, Hastin."

Pain crossed his face, and he let out a slow breath. "Tahlee, please, if nothing else, believe me when I say I would never lie to you about that."

"About that?" She narrowed her eyes. "So what *have* you lied about? To me?"

He didn't move. His gaze didn't leave hers.

"Your name isn't really James, is it?"

He shook his head.

A heavy lump rolled over in her stomach. "It doesn't sound like the name of a thousands-year-old genie. Sorry, djinn. What's your real name, then?"

"I was known as Barqan."

"Interesting name. Far more exciting than James. Did you pick James for yourself?"

"I did. In the 1960s." He chuckled, the sound tired. "I had a thing for James Bond."

She couldn't help but roll her eyes, even as a smile threatened to overwhelm her. "Of course you did."

He grinned.

Her heart tripped over itself. How was he still affecting her this way, given what she now knew about him? He wasn't even *human*, and yet with one grin, she was ready to climb into his lap, fist her hands in his hair, and kiss him stupid.

"Tell me about Barqan," she ordered. Damn it, could her voice sound any huskier?

James lifted an eyebrow at her, let out another sigh, and slumped back beside her. Threading his fingers behind his head, he dumped his heels on the coffee table and stared at his toes. "Barqan was insanely powerful. One of the most revered and feared djinn. The pagans worshipped me as a deity."

"Ah, that accounts for your ego."

He threw her a look.

"S'true." She smiled, a familiar warmth blooming in her stomach. Being in love with James. God, she thought she was done with that. And yet, here she was. Again. "So, Barqan, tell me more. When were you born? Do djinn have parents? I need details, please."

He chuckled. "You've always been inquisitive. Every time."

"Every time?" What did he mean by that?

An unreadable shadow flickered over his face, and then he smiled at his toes. "I was born from the universe."

"Okay, well, if that's not the most enigmatic explanation I've ever heard, I don't know what is."

He laughed. "It's the only explanation I can give you. I wasn't, and then I was."

"So you were born from the universe thousands and thousands of years ago, and what? Spent most of that time granting wishes?"

He grinned at his feet again. "Most of the time, I chillaxed in my own realm."

"Your own what?" Her journalist's brain didn't quite know what to do with that

"My own realm. Djinn don't exist in this realm."

She frowned. Shook her head. Frowned again. "Go on."

Better to hear what he was telling her, digest it, than to think about the implications of it all.

She was having a conversation with a being that wasn't human. About stuff she'd only ever believed was fiction. If she wasn't careful, she'd flip out. Again.

He continued, "We are summoned here. Most of the time, the summoner doesn't realize the situation they've got themselves into. A lot of people have died, trying to navigate the whims of a djinn. Most who summon a djinn don't truly understand the covenant they are entering by doing so. Djinn, by nature, are not that...user-friendly."

A chill rippled up her spine.

He threw her a quick look. "Some of us, however...well, we're not all malevolent beings determined to punish those who dare summon us."

She swallowed. "That's good to hear."

A low chuckle vibrated in his chest. "Of course, if we're provoked, djinn know how to protect ourselves."

"Also good to hear...I think."

He glanced at her. "You're safe with me."

She arched an eyebrow at him.

He laughed again, returning his attention to his feet. "So I was summoned by a sorcerer called Syrin. It doesn't happen much nowadays. Disney has a lot to answer for when it comes to what humans expect of us, and how to contact us. Too many lamps being rubbed, not enough ritual goat sacrifices. But fourteen-hundred years ago, it was very much the thing.

"Syrin was a narcissistic bastard. Gave the term *self-absorbed* new meaning. But he was powerful. The most powerful sorcerer I'd ever encountered. A spell he'd been casting had gone wrong and was slowly killing the people of his village. He couldn't cure them. So, he summoned me and wished for *me* to cure them. He didn't care about them, mind you, but he had a daughter, and he didn't want her to die. Even if he took his daughter away from the village, the curse would still take her life in the most horrific, painful way."

"Rose?"

A calm stillness fell over him. "How do you know that name?"

She blinked. She'd never heard him sound so constrained. Like something was coiled inside him. "I heard you talking to...I don't know, another djinn? Someone I couldn't see in the cinema room, when I discovered you were all see-throughy. You said '*But it backfired, and killed Rose instead.*'"

His eyes closed as a ragged breath fell from him. "I forgot what a steel trap that mind of your is."

Frowning, she studied his still profile. What had just happened? Something. Tension radiated from him. Thick and tangible.

Had Rose been special to him?

Something dark and cold licked through her.

Jealousy.

She pressed her hand to her mouth and looked away. What the flipping hell was she doing feeling jealous? Over a woman from more than a thousand years ago?

What was *wrong* with her?

"Yes, you're right. Rose was Syrin's daughter," he said, voice low, modulated. As if he were deliberating every word he uttered. "When I'd performed the task Syrin asked of me, when our covenant was complete, Syrin was...agitated with me. He decided to cast a spell to erase my existence—his hubris assumed he could—but it went wrong, and it cursed him and Rose instead. She died. As did he."

The sentence left him on steady words. Emotionless words. And yet a lifetime of grief hung in the consonants and vowels. She'd spent enough time interviewing those caught up in corruption to hear it.

"Can't you just...go back?" She frowned at him. "To your realm?"

"A djinn can only be returned to his realm by the one who summoned him. Until that happens..." He stared at his feet. "There have been some who've thought that was a good way to control a djinn, but they learned the painful way that isn't the case." A sly smile—slightly menacing, slightly regretful—pulled at the edges of his mouth. "Remember when I said threatening a djinn isn't wise?"

She nodded.

"But in my case, Syrin was already dead. I couldn't, um... how shall I put this...*encourage* him to return me to my realm, because there was nothing left of him. He'd unmade himself, and in doing so, trapped me here. In mankind's realm."

"And you've been here ever since?"

"Ever since."

Her throat tightened. Her eyes burned. "That's horrific."

He chuckled. "It's not been all bad. I'm still a djinn, which means there's been little hardship in my existence here. I grant wishes—unbeknownst to the wishers—when the mood takes me. And I keep track of the coming and goings of...things."

Again, there was more in that sentence than the simple words. But what? If she asked, would he tell her?

"And I met you," he said, with a gentle nudge of her

shoulder with his. "And that's something I would never change, no matter how many lifetimes..."

He stopped. Rubbed at the back of his neck. Returned his gaze to his feet.

Skin prickling, pulse pounding, she drew a slow breath. "James?"

"Hmm?" He didn't look at her. Didn't move away, but didn't look at her.

"Can I ask a question?"

A wry laugh filled the space between them. "Only one?"

"Only one."

His jaw bunched, and then, with a shaky sigh, he twisted on the lounge to face her. "Shoot."

"Does you being a djinn have anything to do with why you left me, after I told you I was in love with you?"

He studied her, eyes unreadable, body still. "No. No, it doesn't."

It was a lie.

For the first time since meeting him, since knowing him, James had told her a lie. She could see it on his face. Feel it in her soul.

But why?

"James. What aren't you telling—"

"Oi, Hastin?" a male voice shouted from the front of the house. "You'd better not be dead in there."

5

E xtraction spells were always messy.

Wiping his hands on the hem of Mrs. Taylor's dress, Philips smiled up at the woman. "Now, that wasn't too bad, was it?"

She didn't answer.

Tapping her big toe with a finger, he let out a low chuckle, watching as she began to sway.

On the floor, curled loosely on his side, Detective Taylor remained as silent as his wife.

Philips regarded the blood trickling out of the man's empty eye sockets. Admired the way it pooled on the plastic sheet underneath him.

Messy, yes, but worth it.

He returned his smile to Mrs. Taylor. "I'm going to make a cup of tea. Would you like one?"

She didn't answer. Just hung there, drooling, suspended in midair on nothing. Tears leaked from her bulging eyes. Urine dripped from her dangling feet to dribble on her shoes, now discarded on the floor directly below her.

"No tea then?"

Stepping over her husband's inert frame, Philips left his work room, ascended the stairs to the main part of the sprawling house he used as his residence whenever in LA, and headed for his kitchen.

Deep in his mind, a cloud brewed. It would grow bigger, tumultuous. Soon, it would render him catatonic for a few seconds. Vulnerable and mewling. But when the cloud dissipated, everything that had once been in the detective's brain would be in his.

Everything.

Of course, extracting it meant Detective Taylor's brain was now mush, but really, what did the man want with it? His life had been so...so...*mundane*. Boring.

Ineffective.

Waving his hand toward the kettle on the stove, he crossed to the cupboard, removed a teabag from a cannister, and dropped it into his favorite glass cup. The room filled with the shrill *scree* of the kettle boiling a second later, and he silenced it with another wave of his hand.

A cloud of memories, thoughts and knowledge broiled and swelled in his head. His vision blurred for a second, overwhelmed by a maelstrom of images swarming over each other.

There, and then subsiding, leaving a dull ache that gnawed at his mind.

He smiled, filled his cup with freshly boiled water, dunked the teabag a few times, and—breathing in the distinct bergamot aroma—walked back to his work room.

"Still here, Mrs. Taylor?"

He laughed, wandering over to the woman suspended in the air.

Sliding his finger up the back of her leg, he gave her a

slight push, smiling. There was something satisfying in the way she gently swung, as if a coming storm played with her hanging body. A synergy with the building cloud in his head.

His vision blurred again. Images pummeled him. Smothered him. Piled on top of each other, warred with each other.

Taylor having fun with his wife, Taylor chasing down someone running away, Taylor laughing with a group of uniformed cops, Taylor being pushed on a swing, Taylor having his diaper changed, Taylor, Taylor, Taylor...

Hissing, Philips doubled over, holding his teacup tight, gripping his knee with his other hand.

"Whoa Nelly!" He chuckled a few seconds later when the images vanished. "That was a mean one."

Straightening, he took a sip of tea and tapped Mrs. Taylor's toe again. "Did I see a memory of you slapping poor old hubby here in some place that looked like a supermarket?"

Mrs. Taylor swung.

He cast the detective a curious look. "What did you do? Never mind, I'll know soon e—"

The cloud erupted.

He collapsed, every memory and thought Taylor had ever had rushing at him, into him.

He screamed, spine buckling, bowing, limbs doing the same.

He screamed louder and flopped on the floor—and then the room vanished as his brain shut down and soaked up everything.

Everything.

Every...

Philips opened his eyes.

They burned, but the sensation would disappear soon enough. As with the memories and thoughts now in his head, his senses were in the process of advising every nerve and cell in his body that he, too, had experienced everything Detective Taylor had.

Pushing himself upright, he let out a low groan. Curved shards of glass lay scattered next to him, the handle of his tea cup attached to one. The unmistakable scent of tea filled his shaky breath, even though not a drop of the brew was visible.

How long had he been riding the onslaught? How long had he been lost in the cloud?

Long enough for his spilt tea to dry.

Pressing his fingers to his face, he massaged his eyebrows. The contents of Detective Taylor's mind needed a few moment to settle into his own before he could go rummaging through them.

"That was fun," he murmured up at Mrs. Taylor.

Her dangling feet quivered.

He frowned. "Mrs. Taylor?"

Pushing to his feet, he lowered the silent woman with a slow downward stroke of his hand until the tips of her toes kissed the crusty scum of her dried piss on the floor.

Mrs. Taylor's eyes dribbled from their sockets, the gelatinous liquid trickling down her cheeks to join the line of snot along her top lip.

"Fuck."

She'd died. When? During the time his brain was completely absorbing Taylor's? How long was he out for? The binding spell he'd cast to suspend her silently in the air shouldn't have killed her. Unless he'd lost control of it during the onslaught?

"Fuck."

Had she told anyone where she was going? The address?

He had no way of knowing. Her brain was dead, which meant he had no access to it now.

"*Fuck!*" he screamed, smashing his fist into her throat.

Her lifeless body flew across his work room, hit the wall with a wet slap, and dropped to the floor.

Fuck. If she'd told—

"Wait." He shook his head. "Let's see what dear old Detective Taylor knows."

Closing his eyes, he cast the man's mind back two hours. To a few seconds after his wife had taken a call from one very helpful Dr. Quincy.

"Well, that's a relief," he muttered.

According to the detective's memory, Mrs. Taylor hadn't contacted anyone after taking "Doctor Quincy's" call. She'd torn the sheet of paper on which she'd written the address out of the notebook, bundled poor old hubby in a warm jacket despite it being a balmy evening, hurried him out to their Buick Enclave, and driven straight here. No calls were made on the trip, the directions delivered by an impassive Siri from her iPhone.

Good. Once he'd found said phone—no doubt in her purse—and destroyed it, there'd be no evidence to connect the husband and wife to him at all.

"Now..." Settling down onto the floor next to Taylor's body, he swirled his index finger through the sticky blood pooling beneath the detective's head, flicked it at the dead man's eyeless face, and closed his eyes.

And thought of a police station. Specially Detective Taylor's desk in the West LA station. Thought of Tahlee Hope, UK journalist. Thought of a tall man in a dark suit...

...very tall. Taller than me. Huh. It's been a while since I met

someone taller than me. Son of a bitch's eyes are really green. Hell, his hand's cold! But yeah, firm shake. Getting a good vibe from him. Get why he's got a good rep. Yeah, the Brit chick is going to be in safe hands with him and his team. Wonder if the captain has used Guarded Souls' services before or if he called them in on recommendation from higher up. Shit, I've forgotten what his name is. How could I forget...

Philips opened his eyes, smiling as he withdrew from Taylor's memory. "Guarded Souls."

The tall guy in the suit had come from something called Guarded Souls.

Straightening to his feet, he wiped his hand on his chest, smearing what remained of Taylor's drying blood on his skin, and headed for his home office.

"Guarded Souls," he repeated. The name slid over his tongue, like a drop of silver. Something about it sent icy fingers over his scalp.

Arriving in the spacious room he used when he conducted official work from his LA residence, he opened his laptop.

"Guarded," he typed into the search engine, "Souls."

The screen filled with results. Giving the page a quick scan, he clicked on the first link.

And let out a low groan.

"Fuck." A security agency.

So a security agency had taken Tahlee Hope, and no doubt now had her holed up in a safe house somewhere.

But that didn't explain why he'd failed to locate her via magic.

Unless someone at Guarded Souls...

Chest tight, he clicked on the link titled *Team*.

The first headshot was of a man, age indeterminate, with a steely gaze that made Philips's anus clench. There was something menacing about him. Was he the man who'd taken the bitch journalist from the police station? Possibly. He wore a suit. Wore it exceeding well, from what Philips could see from the photo.

"Who are you?" Philips murmured, sliding his attention to the line of text beside the image.

Kade. Founder.

Philips frowned. Just that.

Kade. Was that his first name? Last name?

"Pretentious bastard," he sneered, scrolling down the page to study each headshot of the Guarded Souls team.

Nathanial Knight. Christen North, Daku. Huh, another single-name twat. Idiot. Nimeu Brynn—a chick. What kind of female could work at a protection agency? Especially a small slip of a thing like the woman in the photo? She looked like she should be the poster child for alternative-lifestyle pixies.

He snorted. "Does anyone ugly work at this place?"

Good-looking they all may be, but none triggered anything suspicious. Kade, maybe. But the rest?

He continued to scroll down, getting close to the bottom.

Kitt Newton. James Has—

"—summoned you to save my village, not take my daughter from me!" he screamed, rage and grief shredding his throat. The thatched huts of his village surrounded him, as did the stench of spoiled food, rotting meat, and human refuse.

"You killed Rose, sorcerer." The abomination surrounded by swirling purple smoke narrowed its green eyes. The smoke grew thicker, denser. Angrier. "I tried to save her."

Hate swelled through him and he snarled, even as his heart ripped open. The spell he'd cast to end the creature's existence was devouring him from the inside out. Eating him, killing him. Just as it had Rose.

Rose, oh Rose, my beloved daughter...

"She wasn't yours!" he wailed, pain tearing through him as he stared at the traitorous djinn. "She was not part of our covenant—"

Philips slapped his hands to his face, the sudden light of his office stabbing at his eyes, the smell of death and decay no longer in his breath.

"What the fuck?"

He rubbed his stinging eyes, hunched over, breathless. What the fuck had just happened?

A vision?

No, it felt heavier than that. A...a memory?

He squinted at the harsh light from his desk lamp, his blood thundering in his ears, and then returned his attention to his laptop screen.

To the image of the smiling man called James Hastin.

Nothing. No reaction.

Breath labored, as if he were trying to fill his lung through a pinhole, he studied the image.

There was nothing familiar about Hastin, and yet at the same time, the relaxed smile, the green eyes, the artfully messy hair... It all stirred something deep inside him.

Hate?

Fear?

He narrowed his eyes, glaring at Hastin's image. How could that be? He had no clue who Hastin was. And he feared no one.

No one.

"You killed her, sorcerer..."

The accusation from the vision (memory?) sliced

through his head, and he winced, nostrils filling with the scent of rotting flesh and smoke and death again.

And then it was gone. As though never there.

Of course it was never there. You're in your office, not some ancient, medieval village somewhere.

And yet, he had been.

Hadn't he?

Heart smashing faster in his chest, he stared at the image of James Hastin, branded Hastin's countenance into his brain, and then read the text beside it.

Wishing to be safe? I'm your man.

That was it. Unlike some of the other Guarded Souls' team members, James Hastin clearly thought he was a comedian.

Returning his glare to Hastin's image, he curled his fists.

"Who are you, Hastin?" he whispered.

You know, his own voice whispered back in his head. *It's...*

Philips clenched his jaw. Whoever the fuck the man in the vision was, his name alluded him. And just who the fuck was Rose?

He didn't know. But one thing burned in his soul, one undeniable truth he couldn't explain but believed completely. Whoever this James Hastin was, he had Tahlee Hope.

Which meant he was a walking corpse.

Wishing to be safe? Ha. "No amount of wishing will save you from me, Hastin. Or whoever you—"

Wishing.

Wish.

Green eyes glowering through thick smoke...

Green...

He returned his attention to his laptop, to the image of James Hastin on its screen.

Green eyes. Like the eyes in the smoke in his vision...or his memory.

"Summoned you..." The words from the memory snarled through his mind.

"...part of our Covenant."

Green eyes.

Wishing.

Summoned. Covenant.

Could Hastin be a...a djinn?

A cold finger slid up Philips's spine. A colder smile stretched his lips.

A djinn.

James Hastin was a fucking djinn! Here. In the twenty-first century.

A djinn.

Perfect.

"I'm coming to find you, fucker," he growled, tapping Hastin's smiling face on his laptop screen. "Oh, this is going to be fun."

DAKU STRODE into the safe house, black eyes scanning the room, missing nothing.

"Daku, Tahlee Hope." James waved a hand at Tahlee, and then back to the tall man with the dark hair, dark skin and a dark glower. "Tahlee Hope, Daku."

"Dak." Daku smiled at Tahlee, the action turning his face into something found on the cover of expensive magazines for insanely rich, beautiful people.

"You *can* smile?" James smacked his forehead and reeled back a step. "I didn't think that was possible."

Daku turned a level gaze on him, and James grinned. Dak was one of the scariest beings James had ever encountered, mainly because the dreamwalker could enter anyone's dreams and get up to who-knows-what in there. Anyone's. Human, shifter, vamp, djinn... If an individual slept at any point in time, Daku could slip into their dreams.

What he did in there...

James suppressed a shudder.

Daku was not one to piss off.

Which he currently was.

James was going to kick Kitt's ass when he got out of here. What the hell had the wolf shifter been thinking, sending Daku here?

"Hello, Dak." Tahlee rose to her feet and extended her hand. "Can I assume you're with Guarded Souls?"

Daku bestowed another smile on her. "I am. Coming up to check on Hastin here. Apparently he got cut off during communication with another member of our team, and that team member was worried." He fixed James with a pointed stare. "But clearly, he's fine."

James grinned. "Totally fine. Couldn't be finer."

Apart from the fact barely five minutes ago, he'd told Tahlee what he was.

"In that case, I'll have a beer." Daku's eyes glinted. "Before I head off again."

"You know it's five-thirty in the morning, right?"

Daku didn't blink. "Not back home, it isn't."

Back home. No one at Guarded Souls really knew where "back home" was for Daku, but seeing as he had a slight Australian accent, and could often be heard muttering about the Aboriginal Dreamtime when he was particularly angry, the guess was somewhere from the isolated country south of the hemisphere.

Ask Daku where he came from, and all you got was "Feeling tired, mate?"

James suspected even Kade didn't know. But Daku did things for Guarded Souls no one else could. And, according to Kitt, didn't ask for a cent.

"Okay, beer it is." He arched an eyebrow. "Any particular brand?"

Daku's teeth flashed at him in a quick smile. "Carlton. Dry."

"The expensive stuff." James clicked his fingers, and an icy-cold bottle of the distinct Australian beer filled his hand.

Tahlee gasped.

Daku narrowed his eyes.

James shrugged. "She knows. I told her everything."

Almost everything. Still can't tell her—

Daku regarded him, expression enigmatic, and then accepted the beer. "Here's to knowing everything, then."

He twisted off the lid, raised the beer to Tahlee in a relaxed toast, and drained the bottle in one long go.

"Whoa." She laughed. "That's...umm..."

Daku wiped his lips with the back of his hand, tossed the empty bottle to James, and gave her another smile. "It was nice to meet you, Ms. Hope. I know Hastin here is meant to be looking after *you*, but try to keep him out of trouble if you can."

An unreadable light danced in Tahlee's eyes. "I'll do my best."

Daku chuckled. Actually chuckled. And dropped her a wink.

What the hell? If James didn't know better, he'd think Daku was provoking him.

It's possible he is. Kitt most likely told him how you reacted to seeing Tahlee in Kade's office.

"We're all fine here, Dak. Want me to send you," he raised his hand level with his jaw, fingers poised to click, and wriggled his eyebrows, "back from wherever it is you came from?"

Daku turned on his heel. "Walk with me to the door, Jimmy."

He didn't wait for James to say anything, striding out of the room with the same confidence with which he entered it.

James let out a ragged sigh, clawed his hands through his hair, and threw a sheepish smile to Tahlee. "I'll be back."

"Good. Because you have a question to answer."

He ground his teeth. Shite. He knew she hadn't believed him when he'd said being a djinn had nothing to do with why he'd walked out on her three years ago. He knew she wouldn't stop until she knew the truth. That persistence, that belief in knowing the truth in all situations, defined her. It was one of the things he'd loved about—

Shite.

A cold flush swept over him and his breath caught.

That line of thinking was nothing but dangerous.

"I'll be back," he repeated, hurrying after Daku.

The dreamwalker waited at the front door, bouncing a keychain in one hand, unwavering gaze locked on the abstract painting on the foyer wall. "*Is* everything okay, James?" he asked, voice low, as James approached.

"It's okay. I should have let Kitt know there was nothing to worry about."

Daku lifted an eyebrow. "Nothing to worry about? You revealed what you are to a human. Because she...what? Came upon you projecting yourself into Newton's place? I could be wrong, I'm only a dreamwalker after all, but I think you've got ways of dealing with a compromising situation like that—and they don't involve full disclosure, yeah?"

Full disclosure. Ha.

"I know Hope. She's a dog with a bone when it comes to getting answers."

"Huh. Sure."

"You don't sound convinced."

Daku tapped his finger against James's chest, right over his heart. "I suspect this has something to do with it."

"Sod off, Sandman."

A sly grin split Daku's lips. "Reckon I might go for a walk tonight. See what I stumble upon."

James leveled his own finger at Daku. "You come anywhere near my dreams, and it won't matter how much you wish for the pain to stop. I'll—"

"Mate." Daku held up his hands, shaking his head. "It's okay. I'm fucking with you."

A shaky laugh fell from James. "I don't think I'll ever get your sense of humor, Dak."

"The way I like it. Keeps everyone on their toes." Daku narrowed his dark gaze. "Although I do think you're up to the neck in something. Whatever it is, if you need help..."

"Thanks. Actually, I *do*. Need help. I think..." He stopped. Even contemplating this made his chest tight, let alone saying it aloud.

Daku waited.

"I think there's a sorcerer practicing magic in LA. Dark magic. I could be wrong, but Nim might be able to sense something. Learn something."

"Okay. Learn what?"

"I think..." The band around James's chest grew tighter. "I think whoever it is, they have a connection to the sorcerer who summoned me fourteen hundred years ago."

Connection. That was one way of putting it. "*Is* the sorcerer who summoned me" was another way, but despite what James had felt from Tahlee's laptop bag, he still couldn't bring himself to believe Syrin was resurrected. It wasn't possible. The spell Syrin had cast to unmake James was absolute. Once Syrin died, his existence devoured from the inside out, he no longer existed. Not in the temporal realm, the ethereal realm, nor the Order of Actuality.

He'd erased himself from existence.

The only reason the same didn't happen to Rose was—

"If they do have a connection," Daku asked, "does that mean you'll be able to return to the djinn realm?"

James met the dreamwalker's pinning gaze. "No. Only the original summoner can revoke the summons. Not a descendant."

And Syrin didn't have a descendant. Rose *had* died. Horrifically.

And if the presence you sensed isn't a descendant? If the impossible has happened?

"But there's something not right," he said. "And I need to know what's going on, preferably without whoever the sorcerer is knowing there's a djinn around." A bitter taste filled his mouth and he bit back a growl. "A djinn is like catnip to a sorcerer."

"Glad to hear at least someone finds you attractive."

James snorted. "And there's that wicked sense of humor again."

The corners of Daku's mouth twitched. "Yep."

"You're an interesting individual, Dak. Sure I can't just..." James made a clicking gesture. "I don't know how you got here so quickly, but if I can help get you back, I'm happy to do so."

"Nah, it's all good, mate." Daku jiggled the keys in his hand. "I was, in fact, in the area. Bought a new motorbike a day ago and wanted to take her for a spin on some winding mountain roads."

James narrowed his eyes. What *were* the chances of Daku just being in the area? "Why do I get the feeling Kade's fingerprints are all over this?"

"Don't know what you're talking about, mate. Kitt knew you were in trouble. I'd mentioned to him yesterday I was going for a ride today. He called. He was worried about you."

"He doesn't need to be."

Daku's eyebrows lifted. "You sure about that?"

Before James could answer, the dreamwalker opened the front door. "Okay, I'll track down Nim, fill her in on the possible sorcerer in town and tell her to go talk to Kitt."

"Thanks."

Daku turned back to him, expression enigmatic. "If I were you, mate, I'd click your fingers and erase any knowledge of who you are from the human's mind. Knowing something like that...well, it puts her in more danger than it seems she already is."

And with that, Daku stepped across the threshold and closed the door behind him.

James relocked it, activated the human security system,

and muttered the incantation Nim had set up to reinforce the protective wards around the house.

The fact he'd sensed the presence of a sorcerer on Tahlee's laptop bag meant normal human security measures just wouldn't cut it.

If he was correct, and it *was* Syrin…

"It can't be," he muttered. "It's impossible."

Keep telling yourself that.

A thick pressure clamped around his temples, and he let out a steadying breath. "It's impossible," he repeated.

Preparing himself for the interrogation coming his way, he headed for the living room. Perhaps Daku was right? Perhaps he needed to click his fingers and remove every word he'd told Tahlee from her mind? It'd be easier, that was for sure.

A cold fist twisted in his gut at the thought. He couldn't do it.

Not to Tahlee.

Then how are you going to deal with what's to come? She's going to ask why you left. And you've already failed at lying about it. More than once.

He ground his teeth and rubbed at the back of his neck. He had no clue. And wishing for one wouldn't do him a fat lot of good.

Then this is going to be fun.

He strode back into the living room, forcing a flippant grin to his face. "Want a cup of—"

Tahlee lay stretched on her side, hands tucked beneath her head, eyes closed. The almost inaudible buzz of her soft snores stretched his lips into a real smile. Well, that was one way to sidestep the grilling.

He crossed to the coffee table in front of the couch, crouched until his butt perched on its edge, and watched her sleep. Closed his eyes and let the sounds of her deep breaths roll over him. Pulled breath after breath himself, drawing the scent of her into his being.

How many breaths of her scent had he taken during his existence? Too many to number.

Sometimes, the memory of it was the only thing that kept him going, kept him sane.

An insane djinn was a scary thing. A petrifying thing. His sanity had clung to her scent—delicate, unique, never changing regardless of the perfume or soap she used, at least never changing to him—for so long now, he couldn't remember a time without it. And yet, the memory could never eclipse or replace the real thing.

It had always been this way. From the very first time he saw her.

From the very first time she'd smiled at him. Took his hand. Looked into his eyes and saw his heart. Not just a djinn with the power to deliver almost anything she desired, but a soul, a heart, a being with his own mind, his own wants and hopes, dreams and desires...

Stop that. Now. It's too dangerous. Don't forget why you walked out on her. Don't forget what Syrin did to you upon his death.

Cold, gut clenching, he straightened from the coffee table and clicked his fingers. A soft blanket fluttered into existence, draping over Tahlee's sleeping form. He adjusted it with a gentle touch and left the living room.

He needed to put some distance between them. Needed to clear his head.

Needed to remember the curse Syrin had placed upon him.

Needed, above all else, to deny his love for Tahlee. Love

could never be a part of his existence. No matter how much he wished it could.

He strode through the safe house, wriggling his fingers. Prowling empty rooms.

A hit. That's what he needed. The rush of granting a wish or two.

He stopped walking, knuckles aching as he wriggled his fingers faster.

Just one wish. Anyone's wish. A simple one.

Where was the nearest bar? At this hour of the morning, there was bound to be someone there desperately wanting *something*, craving something. Money, sex, a taxi...

Rubbing the back of his neck, he pivoted on his heel and stared hard toward the direction of the living room.

What was he thinking? Leaving Tahlee alone? What kind of fool was he?

No, he couldn't do that.

Heart a hammer in his throat, he strode back toward where she slept, and then stopped.

If he looked at her right now...

Spinning around, he bit back a groan.

What the fuck should he do?

The events of the morning gnawed at him—Tahlee's return, the taint of Syrin, the darkness deep inside him craving to be released after being repressed for eons...

Shite.

Scraping his hands through his hair, he looked back toward the living room once again.

Erasing Tahlee's memory of his revelation would be so easy. Would make things so much easier...

He ground his teeth. The ancient darkness of his kind broiled and churned inside him, eager for freedom.

A click of his fingers; that's all it would take. One click.

And then, once he'd removed what he'd told her from her mind, he could...could...

"Shite," he growled. He could what? Start again? He couldn't do that.

But you could let her deal with the knowledge she now has? You could let it eat her up, unravel her very notion of reality? You could do that? To her?

But what if Syrin truly *was* resurrected? Being already exposed to the supernatural elements of existence would help her cope with what was sure to come.

"Fark." He clawed at his scalp, breath ragged. Rapid.

Undo it all.

The dark option whispered through his mind.

He *could* undo it all. Everything. Surrender to the potency of his dark magic and undo everything. Rewrite existence from the second she saw him in the pub.

Undo it all until the only thing left is the desperate wishing for—

Head roaring, he dropped his hands from his hair and stared toward the living room.

Tahlee would sleep for a while. She'd had bugger-all sleep through the night—the quick nap on the drive up here was it.

He had to get out of here. For her safety. To keep her safe he *had* to go, even as he knew he shouldn't. She'd be vulnerable alone.

She's vulnerable now. With you, here like this. You know that.

She was.

He'd return to this very moment, this very second, but he had to go. Before what little control he had over his darkness shattered.

Breaths shallow, eyes burning, he thought of a bar. Any

bar. As long as it was open.

And clicked.

The stench of sour beer and stale smoke flowed into his lung. From a shadowy corner, he slowly scanned his new surroundings.

Definitely a bar. A country-themed one, judging by the taxidermized animal heads mounted on the walls and the Randy Travis blaring from an unseen jukebox. And the wood. So much wood.

Wooden floors, wooden tables, wooden seats, wooden bar, wooden stools...

Five patrons sat scattered around the establishment, nursing various alcoholic beverages in various states of consumption. A lone man worked behind the polished-wood behemoth of a bar, drying glasses with an absent expression.

Hurry.

Urgency turned James jittery. Or was it agitation?

Wriggling his fingers, jiggling his arms, and rolling his shoulders, he closed his eyes and tasted the longing in the room.

The dank air was heavy with it. Silent, melancholy hopes swirled about with desperate dreams, craven ambitions and dark cravings.

James released his breath in a slow groan, the despondency like a suffocating shroud. And yet, he'd specifically thought of a bar. Not a café or health club, but a bar. At this time of the morning, those found in a place like this were perfect for his needs.

He flipped through the wants, thoughts, desires and yearnings of those submerged in their unfinished drinks.

A quick hit. That's all he needed. A rush, *the* rush.

He'd be able to face Tahlee, navigate their upcoming

conversation, after a rush. It'd burn off the agitation building in him.

Because you're going to lie to her again?

Or do something even more severe?

So much longing for happiness in here. So many wishes for things to be different.

A strong wave of regret flowed around him, full of an aching need for...something.

James turned to the owner of the regret, the tingle of wish fulfilment already beginning to build in his core.

A man sat alone at a table, tie askew, the suit he wore crumpled, as if he'd slept in it. His fingers wrapped around a tall, almost-full bottle of beer, his eyes half-shuttered, his shoulders slumped.

Even if James hadn't tasted his need, it was clear the man wasn't exactly in the emotional place he wanted to be. Probably not the physical place either.

A fresh wave of regret flowed into James, clearer this time, the longing in the man's heart sharply defined.

James smiled. "Easy done," he whispered.

Ambling over to the table, he grabbed the back of an empty chair, swung it around and straddled the seat, resting his chin on the top of backrest. "You look blue, sir."

The man—in his fifties, with a combover that belonged in a Hall of Fame somewhere—jerked blood-shot eyes up to him. "What? Who..." Any attempt at bravado leeched away, and the man's shoulder's slumped again. "Yeah. Been better."

He returned his stare to his beer. Raised it halfway to his lips then lowered it again. Ragged strips of the bottle's label were scattered over the grimy table, a testament to his tormented state.

James studied him. Beaten and exhausted. The mark of

a man who'd fucked up.

"Whatcha say to her?" he asked, turning up his Bible-belt twang.

The man lifted his head again, surprise melting away to resignation. "That obvious, is it?" He slumped even farther into his chair, turning the bottle around and around on the table with a dejected weariness the likes of which James hadn't seen for a long time.

James let out a sympathetic chuckle. "Been there, my friend." He extended his hand across the table. "James. But my friends call me Jimmy."

Gratitude flittered over the man's face, and he let go of his beer and shook James's hand, his grip firm. "Andrew. Gribble. Andy. That's what the missus—" His voice cracked, and his grip grew limp around James's fingers.

With a warm smile, James gave Andy's hand one more firm pump to complete the age-old ritual. "Think you've messed up too big this time?"

Andy met his gaze, worry and grief eating up his face.

Called her fat. The man's thoughts trickled through James's head, a congested river of bruised dismay and self-loathing. *Told her she needed to cut back on the cupcakes. What was I thinking? She's beautiful. I love her. God, I wish I could take it back. What if she tells me to go? What if she won't let me apologize. Wish I had more courage. Wish I had—*

"Probably," Andy mumbled, lowering his stare back to the bottle in his hand. He plucked at the label again, like it was a scab on a stubborn wound.

The tingle bloomed in James's core. He dragged in a slow breath, studying the top of Andy's head. "Apologizing is hard," he said. "Especially when you know you messed up—and the person you're apologizing to is going to serve you up a new one for being a jerk."

Andy nodded, peeling off more of the label in tiny strips. "Amen."

"But when you *do* apologize..." James let the sentiment dangle in the air.

Andy lifted his attention back to James.

He shrugged, letting his smile turn self-deprecating. "All it takes is a little courage and a lotta love, am I right?"

A dry snort tore at the back of Andy's throat. "If only I had some." The snort turned to a bleak laugh, and he gave James a wobbly smile. "Courage. I've already got the love."

The tingle in James's core turned hotter. He drew up a little straighter on the chair. Preparing himself, eager for what was about to happen.

Here it comes. The rush...

"Courage. It's easy enough to wish for, eh?"

Andy laughed. "Ha. Easy to wish for. Not so easy to have."

"Give it a try. You never know what'll happen. Just say, 'I wish...'" James nudged. Clumsy, sure. Lacking his normal finesse. But getting the job done, feeding the rush, that's what was needed right now. Not finesse. Not subtlety.

Andy snorted again and shook his head with a sad smile. "I wish I had the courage to tell Betsy I was wrong. I wish I could tell her I was an idiot and she's my world, my life. My reason for breathing."

"Done," James whispered "To having the courage to tell those important to us that we're sorry." He fabricated a bottle of beer in his hand and raised it to Andy, riding the soft rush as it coursed through him.

Andy chinked the neck of his bottle to James's. "To having the..." He stopped, a light gleaming in his eyes as he put down the bottle. "You know what? I'm going to."

With a sharp nod, he straightened to his feet. "I love her. And I messed up. I'm going to go home and tell her I love her and I'm sorry."

And without another word, he walked out of the bar.

No, *ran* out of the bar.

James erased the bottle of beer in his hand and rested his chin on the back of the chair, closing his eyes as he rode out the remains of the rush flowing through him. It was a softer ride, a quicker rush. Came from such a hurried wish fulfillment. But still, a rush all the same.

The reason he came here. The reason for leaving Tahlee alone in the safe house.

So why did he still feel so—

A wall of surly contempt smashed into him, a longing for something...heinous.

Opening his eyes, James frowned at the barkeeper.

The man wiped the glass in his hand with languid strokes of a stained dishcloth, looking at the glass but not seeing it. James could glimpse what the man *was* imagining, instead—a deep desire. Could taste the impotency behind that desire. Could feel the hate. The violence...

Just go. Leave. You don't need that kind of rush. You—

Another wall of churlish longing crashed into him. Quickening his blood. Awakening something ancient in him. Older.

Fixing an easy smile on his face, he straightened from the chair and wandered over to the bar. Rapping his knuckles on its wood surface, he gave the man a wink when he looked up. "Gin and tonic. No ice." He tapped the bar in a jaunty tune and grinned. "I'm celebrating."

The barkeeper slung the dishcloth over his shoulder and began to fix James's drink. "Something good happen?"

"Better than good." He thickened his Southern accent.

"My boss just got sacked. Uppity bitch thought she was better than me."

The barkeeper grunted, contempt twisting his face as he handed James his gin and tonic. "Lucky son of a bitch."

James lifted a curious eyebrow. "You don't like your boss?" He slapped the bar again, twisted about to bestow the place an overt inspection, and then locked his stare with the barkeeper's again. "Tell me all about it. Is your boss here?"

Another grunt, this one ripe with disgust. "The bitch that owns this place wouldn't be caught dead in here. Too busy sipping mojitos on her fucking yacht."

James made an oh-boy-that-sucks noise in the back of his throat, encouraging the man's subconscious desire to unload.

The barkeeper snorted. "Ain't that the truth. The cunt expects me to work 'round the clock, but rides my ass constantly from her throne at the marina."

"She's rich?"

"Married an old codger. He bought her this place as a wedding present. Supposedly he proposed to her here."

So easy to prod and knead the man's desires. So easy to get him to talk...

James pulled a face, sharing the man's disgust of the situation. "Urgh. Have you met him?"

A cold laugh spilled from twisted lips. "Yep. Spat in his drink once. *His* kind don't deserve..." He trailed off, dropping his eyes away. Confusion tainted his longing.

"Ah," James whispered, leaning forward a little. "I get what you mean." He tapped the side of his nose. "You can't quit?"

"Nope. Up to my ass in bills. My ex is sucking me dry in alimony, my kid is constantly begging for stuff for school.

If I had money..." He looked up at James and smiled. The smile of a man lost in a dream. "If I had enough money, I'd buy this fucking place and bulldoze it to the ground. Right in front of my cunt boss and her..."

A word screamed in the barkeeper's head, so loud James almost winced. A reprehensible word from a vile, bigoted mind. A repellant word.

"...husband," the barkeeper finished with a secretive smirk.

James wanted to smash his fist into the man's nose. "Wish you were rich?" he said instead, resting an elbow on the bar. He held the man's stare. Imprisoned it.

"So fucking rich I didn't have to work." The barkeeper sniggered. "The only joy I get outta coming here is getting to spit in everyone's drink when they're not watchin'."

A perverse heat began to flow through James. His blood surged through his veins in a prickling river. Every molecule in his human form quivered, charged with the oncoming rush about to hit his ethereal form.

He swallowed, swirling his untouched glass in a slow circle on the counter even as he smiled at the man on the other side. A second rush built within him. Dark and tainted by the man's hate and resentment.

But a rush all the same. A potent one.

He closed his eyes for a second, savoring the power, the energy, the ride...

"How much money *would* you wish for?" he asked, looking at the bartender again.

"So much I'd drown in it." The barkeeper gave him a voracious smile. "I wish I had so much money, I fucking drowned in it."

The intangible wall hit James. Slammed into him. Flowed through him. He thrummed. Rode the heady frenzy. Letting go of his glass, he smiled at the man and dipped his head in a single nod. "Done."

The bartender blinked. And then laughed. "I like you. You get it. The next one's on the house. Fucking elitist, rich feminazis, and fucking bl—"

He burped loudly. Frowned. Belched again and rubbed at his stomach.

Coughed.

"You okay?" James asked, the fading remnants of the rush licking at him.

The man's frown turned to a grimace. "I think..."

He belched again—and a quarter fell from his mouth.

James raised his eyebrows. "Hey, neat magic trick. Maybe you should quit being a barkeep and become a magician?"

The man gaped at the quarter on the counter, glistening with spit and bile. A wobbly laugh bubbled up from his throat. "Y-yeah. Yeah, maybe I sh—"

He burped again. Grabbed his stomach, staggering back a step. And another. His ass bumped into the shelves of spirits behind the bar. Bottles chinked and rattled.

"You don't look too good, dude," James commented.

The barkeeper—now doubled over, both hands planted on his shaking knees—looked up at him.

And heaved.

A river of quarters spewed from his mouth, splashing to the floor.

And then more.

And more.

They poured from him. Didn't stop. Became a torrent of coins, and then notes. Crumpled and damp and smelling of stomach acid.

And the more he threw up, the thicker the river of

coins and bills became. Spilling over the floor. Piling up around his feet. His ankles. His calves.

"Yeah," James said, voice calm. Almost indifferent. "You *really* look like you made a bad choice somewhere."

Another geyser of coins. Splattering onto the wet pile already at his knees. Knees that shook.

Coins. A tsunami of them, gushing from his mouth. Spurting from his nose.

Somewhere in the bar, someone coughed.

James flicked a glance behind him.

No one was paying any attention. One of the patrons— a woman nursing what looked like a vodka and cranberry juice—turned her back on the bar completely.

The tinkle and chink of coins falling onto a dense mountain of money drew James's attention back to the bar.

The barkeeper collapsed onto the slick pile. Didn't look up. Floundered against the ocean of wet currency still spewing from his mouth.

"Having fun?" James asked.

The barkeeper didn't answer. Didn't respond.

Giving the counter a soft rap with his knuckles, James dropped a wink at him. "Drowning in money. When will you lot ever learn?"

The barkeeper reached a quaking hand toward him.

James smiled, holding the man's fading stare. "Perhaps you'll think twice before being a misogynistic, racist prick, eh?"

He raised his hand, fingers poised. "Oh—and don't ever spit in anyone's drink again."

The sharp report of his click shattered the air.

The money vanished. All of it.

Just as James translocated back to the safe house.

6

How the flipping hell could she let herself fall asleep?

Maybe because, apart from the brief catnap driving here, you've been awake for almost thirty-six hours?

Probably. The fact she'd fallen asleep the moment she allowed herself to sit still wasn't surprising, just frustrating.

With all the enthusiasm of a sluggish sloth, Tahlee pushed herself up into a sitting position and scowled at the empty living room.

"Jet lag sucks," she muttered, rubbing the heel of her hand against her left eye before squinting at her watch.

10:42 am.

Great, so she'd been asleep for an hour. A power-nap. James probably thought he'd escaped their conversation about—

James.

James was a genie.

Her breath burst from her, and she slumped back into the lounge, the reality of what she'd seen, experienced, discovered last night crashing over her again.

A heavy pressure settled on her chest. Her blood pounded in her ears.

Her ex was a genie. A djinn. Ancient. Powerful.

Seriously powerful.

Magically powerful.

"Oh boy." She pressed the heels of her hands to both eyes this time and shook her head. "Okay, process this. Again. So, he's a magical being. Magical beings are a thing. At least, genies are. So what? Doesn't let him off for being a massive jerk three years ago."

Her stomach clenched at her pep talk.

She'd been in love with a magical being. She was *in* love with a magical being. A jerk magical being who could probably make her disappear if he wanted to.

But he won't.

Every fiber in her body knew that. Jerk he may be, but he wasn't evil.

Are you sure?

Yes. She was. Whatever was going on with James, she knew his heart. From the first minute, the first second, she'd known him. As if she'd known him her whole life.

Longer, even.

Which wasn't possible, but the way she felt nonetheless.

Of course, that didn't excuse him for walking out on her mere minutes after her declaration of love. Okay, yes, she understood why he didn't just go, "Hey, I'm a djinn. Probably best we don't take this to the next level." But to leave? Without even a goodbye?

Dropping her hands, she glared around the living room. Djinn or not, he had some explaining to do. If he thought otherwise...

"James?" she called.

Silence.

She frowned. Refused to let her heart thump up into her throat.

"James?"

Her voice bounced around the room, unanswered.

No. No, he hadn't done this to her *again*. He hadn't.

Had he?

Pushing herself to her feet, she walked from the living room, heading deeper into the house. The last time she'd gone searching for James, everything had been turned upside-down. Her mind had been blown.

What would she find now?

"It better be a flipping unicorn," she muttered.

The first three rooms she searched were empty—two bedrooms and a space that looked like it was set up to be an office. The door to the home cinema stood open, and she approached it, heart resuming its battle to get into her throat.

Empty. Not even a unicorn. Or a horse with an ice cream cone stuck to its forehead.

"Well, that's something, I guess."

So where was he?

"James?"

More silence.

She ground her teeth.

Who the hell had a safe house so big? How much flipping money did Guarded Souls make to afford a house like this to hole up clients?

Stomping away from the cinema room, she headed back through the living area, and into what looked like a short, narrow hallway leading to a closed double-door entry.

Another bedroom?

Unicorn stable?

"With my luck, it'll be a magical portal to another dimension where journalists are the bad guys."

Throat growing tighter, she opened one of the doors.

"Wow," she breathed.

A massive bedroom was on the other side, almost as large as the living room. In the middle, beneath a row of three large skylights, a low Japanese-inspired bed dominated the space. Its red and black silk duvet looked priceless, as did the Japanese paintings on the walls.

It was, quite simply, a stunning room.

And unlike all the other rooms, *not* empty.

James stood at the floor-to-ceiling windows on the far side of the room, looking out at a dense redwood forest, his back to the door, his hands pressed to the glass.

Tahlee stopped, studying him.

His fingers flexed and flattened, over and over, as if he were trying to claw his way through the smooth glass. His shoulders bunched. He shook his head, an almost imperceptible side-to-side motion, before he curled one hand completely into a fist and thumped it loudly against the window.

She jumped, a soft gasp escaping her lips.

In a blur of bruised-purple smoke, he was in front of her, nostrils flaring, eyes pure white.

"James?" she yelped, staggering back a step.

A raw sound tore from him, his eyes shimmering back to green, and he dug his fingers into his hair, retreating a step. Another.

"It's better you not be in this room right now, Hope," he ground out, turning away.

Grief choked his voice. And hate.

She'd heard it enough throughout her career to recognize it now.

She'd never heard it in James's voice before. It tore her apart.

"Talk to me, James," she ordered, chest tight. "What's wrong?"

He shook his head, fingers still in his hair, and walked back to the window. No, almost stumbled back to the window, at times solid, at times a smoky blur.

"You shouldn't be here."

An icy finger traced up her spine. She frowned, watching as he planted his palms to the window again. Tension hunched his shoulders.

"Why not?" she asked. A tornado of butterflies swirled in her stomach.

He won't hurt you. You know he won't hurt you.

His right hand curled into a fist on the window. The air seemed to vibrate as a faint purple smoke eddied around him.

"James?" She took a step forward. She refused to be scared. Not of James. Never of James.

His shoulders bunched more. "There's a darkness to all djinn. Part of our creation. We are born from want and desire, good *and* bad."

"Okay." Her voice scratched at her dry throat.

His head dipped as a raw sigh tore from him. "While you slept, I found...a place. Found someone who wanted something. Granted his wish."

The icy finger previously trailing up her spine sank into her heart. "What...what was his wish?"

He pulled in a deep breath, the sound of it rough in the quiet room, and turned his head a little. Enough for her to see his profile. To see the muscle in his jaw knot. "It doesn't matter. He got what he asked for."

She swallowed. What did that mean? "Is he..." Oh God, did she really want to ask this?

No, but she had to.

"Is he still alive?"

The question fell in the silence between them.

"Yes. A djinn cannot kill the wisher. Even if we want to." He turned back to the window, fist unfurling until his fingers splayed over the glass. "But I let the darkness out."

She blinked. Took a step back. "Darkness? I don't... What do you mean, you let the darkness out?"

"Almost *all* magic is born from darkness," he said, without turning, his voice low. "Regardless of its origin. It may reside in the magical being or the practitioner as little more than a kernel, but it *is* the beginning of it all for them. The fight for those who value humanity and life is to repress that darkness, ignore its allure and potency. A djinn's darkness however, is more terrible and powerful than most. We are beings born from concentrated want, after all. Such selfish emotion can only give birth to venal power. If unleashed, if fed, a djinn's darkness can destroy the fabric of reality."

"Destroy—" She stopped, rattled. Destroy *reality*? Could anything be that powerful? Could James? "So you let your...darkness out on a person?" She licked her lips, her throat dry. "Did he deserve it?"

A short, humorless laugh shook his shoulders. "I've prided myself on always giving the wish that's deserved."

"Will he be okay?"

"Yes."

"Will you?"

He turned, and Tahlee gasped, the haunted torment burning in his face shearing through her heart.

"Are you in control now?" she whispered. "Of your darkness, I mean?"

His eyes closed as his expression twisted with grief. "Yes. I've controlled mine for centuries. Because of one person. One pure, beautiful person. Until tonight, I controlled my darkness to be better for her."

Tahlee's head roared.

"For who?"

Rose. The name slipped through her mind, wrapped in a gossamer-thin rope of jealousy.

"For you, Hope," he whispered.

"For me?"

For centuries?

That didn't make sense. She hadn't known him that long.

And yet, she'd always felt like she'd known him forever.

A cold prickle razed her skin. "James...have you ever used your magic on me?"

His jaw bunched. "I've never used my djinn magic on you, Tahlee Hope."

She swallowed. Something itched at her at his answer, but what? "Why me?" she asked. "I mean, if you'd never met me, would you be...a dangerous djinn?"

A wry smile pulled at his lips. "All djinn are dangerous."

"Answer the question, James."

He ducked his head and let out a shaky breath. "The darkness is powerful, Tahlee. And addictive. It's raw and absolute and freeing. And until I met you, I believed it was my only existence."

"Until you met me?" She frowned, heart thumping in her throat. "In the pub in Piccadilly?"

His jaw knotted again. "Until I met you. You changed everything for me. From the very moment you smiled at me, the darkness...it lost its allure. From the moment I met you, I controlled it. Always for you. Only for you."

"Why?" It was a stupid question, but the only one she could ask. A creature with powers beyond her comprehension stood before her, telling her she was the reason for denying the malevolence within. What chance did she have of processing that?

He closed his eyes, that sheepish grin she loved so much playing with his lips. "I am better with you. I want to be better *for* you. I like who I am with you. Because of you."

Oh wow.

The sheepish smile faded. "But tonight, I let the darkness out. I had to. The torment over what I'd brought to your life, it's almost destroying me. If I could undo my own existence I would do so without hesi—"

She closed the distance between them, took his face in her hands and silenced him with a slow kiss. Ended the words before they could tear her apart. A life without James in it? A world without him? No, it was too horrific to consider.

She kissed him.

Gave him her heart.

How many times had she done that in their time together? Every time she'd kissed him, she gave her heart to James.

She kissed him, wanting to take away his pain. It didn't matter that he'd hurt her years ago. Not at that moment. They'd sort that out. Later.

It didn't matter he was a magical being thousands of years old with more power in his pinkie than she could ever imagine.

Right now, the important thing was taking away the pain she could see in his eyes. The grief she could see eating up his soul.

She parted her lips and sought out his tongue, offering and asking and leading and surrendering.

He groaned—this powerful being—and wrapped his arms around her and kissed her back. Pulled her closer to his body with a gentle hug, as if scared she would stop him.

No way.

Three years she'd ached for his kisses. Three years she'd longed to hear his laugh, see his smile. Feel his gaze and turn to find him watching her, eyes twinkling with mirth and happiness and delight.

She'd never kissed him to take away pain or anger in all their time together. They'd never had a need for make-up sex. He'd never brought sorrow into their life together until he'd left it. From the second he'd entered her life, until he'd left so unexpectedly, he'd given her laughter and joy and contentment, and she kissed him now to remind him of that.

To drive away his darkness.

She smoothed her hands down his back and poured her soul into their kiss.

A part of her mind kept whispering that she wasn't kissing a human, but she didn't care. He was James. *Her* James. And human or not, he was hurting, and she would do whatever she could to take his pain away.

Kissing him may not make him feel human, she didn't want it to, but it sure as hell would let him know she cared.

Loved him.

God help her, she always would, no matter what he was.

She sought his tongue again, stroking her own against it. He groaned, his arms drawing her closer still to his body. She melted into him, exactly where she wanted to be. Since his vanishing act three years ago, she'd convinced herself she was too busy to date again. Too busy for any kind of relationship. She had her vibrator and her work. She didn't need anything else.

Kissing him now, being held by him, holding him, his heat seeping into her, his hands exploring her back, her hips, her arse, she knew her celibacy had had nothing to do with how busy she was. She'd wanted no one else but James.

No one else but James would suffice.

Scary as it was, it was a simple fact. She'd deal with it later, just as she would deal with his reason for abandoning her—whatever it might be.

Now...

Moving her hands between their chests, she popped open the buttons of his shirt and slid her fingers over his smooth skin.

He groaned again, the raw sound vibrating through her body as he tore his mouth from hers and gazed into her eyes. "I wish..."

Heart thumping, she rose up onto her tiptoes and nipped at his chin. "Wish what?"

Squeezing her arse, he let out a shaky laugh. "So many things."

"Tell me."

His nostrils flared. "Can I kiss you instead?"

"Why?"

"Because it's my second favorite thing in existence to do. Always has been."

"What's your first?"

His lips twitching, he hauled her off her feet and placed her on the massive bed.

"Oh." She combed a hand through his hair and pulled him down to her, wrapping one leg around his hip to draw their groins closer together. "That."

He shook his head, eyes smoldering. "Being with you in any and every way. *That's* my favorite thing in existence. Just...being with you."

"Then why did you leave?" she whispered.

Instead of answering, he kissed her. And kissed her. And kissed her. Gentle, long, thorough, hungry, passionate kisses.

Kisses that moved from her mouth, journeyed down her chin, her neck, along her collarbones, and back to her lips again.

Kisses that awoke in her an unfathomable ache, an endless longing, an infinite desire.

She moaned and tugged at his shirt. "Take this off," she ordered against his lips.

He didn't move, didn't break their kiss, but suddenly her hands were splayed against bare skin.

She gasped, tugging his head up with a fistful of hair. "You just genie'd yourself shirtless."

"I did."

"Do it to me."

An unreadable light flickered in his eyes. "Are you sure?"

"Do it to—"

Her shirt vanished, the warmth from his naked torso pressing to hers.

She gasped again, a tingle of excited lust sinking into her center. "Naked. I want to be naked with you."

His nostril flared again. "Is that what you *wish* for?"

She pressed her hips upward, aligning their groins closer together. "I wish we were both naked right now."

The room's air kissed her suddenly naked body. The only thing still on her was her necklace. "Holy crap," she breathed, rolling her hips. His skin slid against hers, warm and familiar and perfect. "Could you *always* do this? When we were together?"

He smiled. "Yes."

"And I wasted that power?"

He laughed, the thick shaft of his erection rubbing against her folds. "I didn't think it was all *that* bad without the whole phenomenal djinn power to lend a hand."

She grinned, tightened her thigh around his hip and drew his head down to hers with a steady hand. "It was the best I've ever had."

That enigmatic light flickered in his eyes again, and then he kissed her.

She gave herself over to the moment. To his kisses, his laughter, his smile, his touch. She rode the wave of pleasure they awoke in her, and when it began to build to a breaking point, she rolled him onto his back and straddled his hips, pinning his wrists to the bed on either side of his head.

He groaned out a laugh, like he used to every time she took charge, and pushed his hips upward. "Now *this* is power," he said.

"And it's mine to wield." She wriggled on his hips, squeezing his sides a little with her thighs before leaning forward and brushing her nipples over his chest.

"Shite, Hope..." His eyes closed. His erection pulsed against her soft heat. "I'm yours. Always have been."

For centuries...

His earlier words tickled through her mind again. Teased something deeper. Itched at her.

For centuries. He'd said he'd controlled his darkness for centuries, for *her*. To be better for *her*. But that made no sense. How could it? She'd only known him since—

"Always will be," he murmured, opening his eyes. They glowed. Iridescent white. "Only yours."

A tight shiver claimed her. Her nipples beaded. Her core flooded with liquid heat. She lowered her head and kissed him.

She'd ask him about it later. After.

Right now, she just wanted what she'd had three years ago.

She moved her lips and tongue over his, demanding more. Demanding everything.

He gave it to her.

A shudder of raw pleasure rocked her and she slid her hands down his arms, to his chest. The rapid beat of his heart beneath her palm ignited a base delight in Tahlee, and she lifted her head, smiling down at him, breaths shallow. "Do you have a heart like this in your realm?"

His eyes closed as he pushed his hips upward, grinding his length to the junction of her thighs. "Ever the journalist," he groaned, part protest, part mirth.

She wriggled her hips, loving the way he groaned again. "Ever the journalist. Do you mind if I record your response?"

Laughing, he gazed up at her. "Now that was something we never did, make a sex tape."

"Missed opportunity," she agreed, reveling in the way

his heartbeat quickened against her hand when she pinched his left nipple. "I have no clue where my phone is, otherwise I'd open the camera app and hit record."

Devilish mischief flashed in his eyes—green and human once again. "I could conjure up a video camera and tripod if you like."

A greedy flutter bloomed into life in the pit of her belly at the thought. "Tempting."

He arched an eyebrow. "Or I could just do this?"

He flipped her onto her back, capturing her laughing squeal with a hungry kiss.

"I like that," she said when he raised his head. She wrapped her legs around his hips, locking her ankles together at the small of his back. "And that," she murmured as he nibbled a path down the side of her throat.

"I'm glad." He flicked his tongue into the shallow hollow at the base of her throat. "And to answer your earlier question, yes. And no."

She let out a chuckle at his ambiguous statement, and then moaned as he moved his mouth to the tip of her right breast. "Ela...elaborate," she ordered, tangling her fingers in his hair as he drew her flesh deep into his warm, wet mouth.

He *hmm*'d around her nipple, sending a ribbon of tight pleasure through her, and then lifted his head a little. His eyes glowed white for a second then they were green again. "Are you sure I can't distract you with this?" He dragged his thumb over her moist nipple, pupils dilating as she sucked in a shaky breath.

"Why not both?" she rasped, tightening her legs around his hips. "You tell me all about your djinn existence as you make insanely intense love to me?"

"I like that idea. Let's do that.."

She laughed, and then moaned again as he captured her nipple once more with his mouth and sucked. "Oh yeah."

He *hmm*'d again, longer this time, drawing deeper on the puckered tip, before lifting his head again and blowing on her wet flesh. His erection pulsed at the junction of her thighs, sending another ribbon of pleasure though her.

"In my realm," he said, brushing her nipple with the pad of his thumb, "a djinn's heart is *all* there is. We exist not as a substantial form, but as a potent nebulous force." He nipped his way across her chest to her other nipple, flicked his tongue over it, and then worshipped it with his mouth for long, luxurious moments.

"S-so when do you...oh boy, that's good..." She writhed beneath him, fist balling tighter in his hair. "When do you...take on human form?"

He continued to adore her nipple for a heartbeat, before releasing it with a pop and gazing down at her. "When we're summoned."

"You pick the way you look, or is it just the way you are when you get here?"

"I pick. I create my human visage." Another flash of white in his eyes.

She arched beneath him, raking one hand down his back as she ground her sex to his. "I like your pick. You did well."

His nostrils flared and he let out a groaning chuckle. "You've told me that be—" He stopped, eyes completely white.

"Told you what—" she began, before, in a blur of deep purple smoke, he repositioned himself on the bed, his head between her spread thighs.

His white eyes held hers for a split second down the length of her body, and then his tongue found the epicenter of her pleasure.

The rest of her words, her question, got lost in the waves of sensation crashing through her.

Bunching the bed's duvet in her hands, she planted her soles on his shoulders and arched into his mouth, his name falling from her in a raw groan.

"Whoa," she panted, gazing blankly up at the ceiling. "I forgot how good you were at this."

He laughed against her heat, a low, throaty reprimand, and then propelled her closer to the edge of eruption.

The air swirled around them, misty and purple. "Is this you?" she asked on a wobbly breath. "This...this smoke?"

Another laugh, this one accompanied by soft, invisible caresses along her inner thighs, breasts and nipples. No, not invisible. The smoke... Tendrils of smoke stroking and teasing her skin.

"Does that answer your question," he murmured, eyes glowing white.

He returned his mouth to her sex as a tendril of misty purple played over her rib cage, across her stomach, and up to her breast, flowing over her distended nipple with increasing pressure.

Wow.

"Wow," she breathed, the dewy touch at once surreal and exciting.

Lifting his head, he blew on her wet folds. "Wow is a start. Tell me what you wish for, Hope."

She laughed. "What I *wish* for? Are you kidding?"

He shook his head, eyes burning white.

Liquid electricity shot through her, sinking into her core. "Um... I don't..."

"Hit me with it." His lips curled. "Your most secret sexual wish."

"So if I say, I wish for an orgasm so amazing I see stars, I'll have an orgasm so amazing I'll see stars?"

He nodded, a naughty smile playing with his lips.

She laughed again. "Sure. Alright then. James, I wish for an orgasm so amazing, I see stars."

He raised his hand in front of his face and clicked. "Done."

It began deep in the very core of her being. Bloomed out to the base of her spine. Radiated through her lower body. Ebbing and swelling and rolling through her; a pleasure unlike any she'd ever experienced. Bone deep, as if every fiber of her body, every molecule had suddenly become a vessel for concentrated pleasure.

She gasped, and then moaned and arched and clawed at the duvet. Heels digging into the bed, she slammed her hips upward. Tossed her head from side to side.

"Oh God," she whispered, as another onslaught of intense pleasure rolled through her. Her vision blurred. Her body trembled. A distant part of her mind recognized James wasn't touching her. Nothing was touching her. The pleasure erupting through her came from...from...somewhere, but not his hands or tongue or—

"Oh God!" she cried again as another tsunami of pleasure crashed over her. She bucked her hips, her vision blurring into points of bright, swirling colors. "*Oh God!*"

The colors grew brighter. Brighter. Until, at the zenith of the most intense orgasm of her life, they burst into twinkling stars so dazzling, she cried out again and closed her eyes.

Pulse after pulse of pleasure filled her body, turning her cries into whimpers. She gripped the duvet, spent and exhausted, until the pulses faded away, leaving her gasping for breath and limp with bone-deep sexual satisfaction.

"Okay," she mumbled, too drained to articulate anything. "That was...wow."

"You're welcome."

She opened her eyes at James's chuckled response.

Kneeling between her spread thighs, hands resting loosely on his own, he winked. "And you thought you'd have to rub something to get that level of—"

She grabbed a pillow from above her head and threw it at him.

It hit him in the chest, and he laughed.

"That was insane," she said, pushing her hair from her face. Flipping hell, she was so sweaty.

"Good though?"

Shoving herself into a half-sitting position, she nodded. "You better believe it."

He preened.

She lifted an eyebrow. "But..."

"But?"

"There was something missing."

He frowned. "What?"

She smiled, moved onto her knees and threaded her fingers into the hair at his nape. "You."

Realization flickered in his eyes. "Ah. Well, if you want me to do it the old fashion, no-djinn-power way..."

"That's exactly what I want," she whispered, tugging his head to hers. "You, moving inside me. Making me come with your—"

He kissed her.

And she kissed him back, flattening him to his back on the bed, straddling his hips once more.

He made love to her mouth with his tongue and lips.

He explored her body with his hands. She let her fingers roam over his chest, his ribs, his hips. She cupped his balls, and squeezed his cock, loving the way he groaned into her mouth. The way his length grew thicker in her grip.

Loved the way his breath mingled with hers as their kiss turned to playful nips of each other's lips.

Loved the way their slick skin slid together.

"I want you inside me, James," she whispered against his lips, capturing his wrists and pinning them to the bed beside his head once again. "I want to come with you. Together. Like we used to."

"I want that too."

Her heartbeat quickened. "I'm still on the pill. But do you want...need a condom?"

He let out a low chuckle. "Part of the phenomenal djinn power...no need for one. That kind of thing I can control with a simple thought."

"Well then, in that case..." She shifted on his hips and, holding his stare, slowly took his length deep into her body.

His glowing eyes fluttered closed. His body shuddered. "My Tahlee, my Hope..." He groaned. "My—"

He groaned again, tossing his head to the side as he slammed his hips upward, driving deeper into her.

She released his wrists, captured his hands with hers, and threaded their fingers together, palm to palm, as waves of pleasure rolled through her.

Driving her closer and closer to a release she didn't want yet.

It had been too long without him, too many long, lonely nights. Too many empty moments.

"James," she rasped. Other words tumbled over each other in her head, words of lust, of confusion. Of longing and love. "James," she repeated, refusing to allow them out.

Not yet.

After.

Later.

He squeezed her hands—and suddenly they weren't in the bed, but in a cloud of purple, the only friction from their bodies moving together in perfect rhythm.

The exquisite change detonated her orgasm. Or maybe it was the raw desire burning in James's shimmering white eyes? She cried out, tendrils of purple smoke caressing her naked body as James thrust into her, his hands roaming her ribs, her hips, his mouth doing the same to her breasts and throat and lips.

A second orgasm shuddered through her, and as she lost control of her body, James threw back his head, his strokes wild and erratic.

And then the smoke was gone, and they were back on the bed, bare limbs tangled and slicked with sweat, fingers threaded.

Pleasure crashed over her, unmade her, and she bucked, screaming his name. Begging him not to stop, to keep going, to never stop loving her.

"Oh God, James!" she cried. "I...I... God, James..."

He released her hands, hips thrusting faster, and buried his face into the side of her neck, his length driving deeper into her. Deeper. Until all rhythm shattered.

He filled her. She felt it.

"I'm yours," he groaned against her neck. "I'm yours. My Tahlee. My Hope. My Rose."

Rose.

The name whispered through her head.

And as it echoed, she no longer lay on a bed in a room,

but instead stretched on lush grass, the sweeping sky blue and cloudless overhead, the sweet smell of wild daisies and lilies in her breath as she smiled up at James—*Barqan* —and brushed her fingers over his jaw.

Barqan. My Barqan. I love you. I love you.

His green eyes held hers as he thrust inside her. *I love you, my Rose. You are my one wish, my one Hope. I love you...*

Tahlee gasped.

The blue sky evaporated, the grass disappeared, replaced by the bedroom ceiling and mattress once again.

"Rose..." James whispered, looking down at her. Torment filled his eyes, once again green and human. "Tahlee."

Tahlee stared at him, the throbbing pulse of her climax fading, the pounding of her heart like a canon in her throat. "What...what did...did you just..."

His eyes shut for a second, and then he slowly withdrew from her, retreated from the bed, and clicked his fingers beside his hip.

His clothes reappeared on his body, at the exact moment hers did as well.

"What just happened, James?" she whispered as she scrambled into an upright position. "What was that? What... Who *is* Rose? Am I..."

She couldn't say it. It was silly.

No. It's real. That was real. You know it. In your soul, you know it. Which means...

She stared at him. At James.

Barqan. His name is Barqan. And you are—

"Rose." The name fell from her lips on a breath. "I'm Rose. Aren't I?"

"Yes." His expression conveyed nothing. "And no."

"What the flipping hell does that mean?" Oh God. Oh God, was the room spinning, or was she?

He took a step closer to the bed, but stopped when she shook her head. "Not a step closer, James, until you explain what the hell is going on."

"Okay." He rubbed at the back of his neck, eyes closed, and then let out a ragged sigh. "Okay."

Opening his eyes—still green; *phew*—he dropped his hand and gave her a wry smile. Not sheepish, but wry. "Fourteen hundred years ago, you *were* Rose. I met you when Syrin—your father, the sorcerer—summoned me in 618 A.D. to save his village. We fell in love. It's dangerous for a djinn to fall in love, it makes us weak. Vulnerable. But I didn't care, because I was more *real* with you. Not just a creature who could deliver. You didn't want anything from me, except to be with me. Asked nothing of me, except my smile.

"When your father discovered us, he was furious. No miscreant, mystical creature would be with his beloved daughter. It mattered not to him that you loved me. He cast a spell. Tried to unmake me. Unfortunately for him, such a spell can never work on a djinn...so it sought out the closest human soul to attack. Yours. And the spell was so dark and malicious, it also attacked *him*."

She swallowed.

Every word played out in her mind like a faint silent movie of the event. She saw a petite woman with long dark hair. She saw a tall, thin, wild-eyed man with a hooked nose and scraggly gray hair screaming at James.

James, who looked the exact same as he did now except for his attire.

She saw the thin man—*Father*—throw his hands

toward James—*Barqan*. She saw the woman—*herself, Rose* —scream and fall to the ground.

She swallowed again, and shook her head. "So if this man, Syrin...if he killed me, how am I here now? Reincarnation? I don't believe in it. There's no such thing."

For a second, his wry smile turned playful. "Just as there's no such thing as genies?"

She blinked.

He dragged a hand through his hair. "Before Syrin's spell could end your life, before it could *unmake* you, I defied djinn law by casting and granting a wish of my own." Pain etched his face. "When I return to my own realm, I will suffer greatly for that wish. But I don't care."

"What was it?" she whispered. "Your wish?"

That wry smile returned. "For you to continue to live."

Her stomach clenched. She touched the pendant at her neck, but for the first time, its tiny gold shape didn't ease anything.

"But as is the way with djinn's granting wishes," he went on, eyes growing distant, "sometimes what you get isn't what you were wanting. I wished for you to live, so we could be together. Instead, you died, as did Syrin."

"Then how..."

His eyes met hers. "You—Rose—were reincarnated. Ten years after you died, I felt your soul return to this realm and found you in Rome. You were born to a happy, loving family, and I made sure you and your family were safe. From a distance. When you died of illness at the age of eleven, I cried alone. And then, twenty years later, you were reincarnated again in what's now known as Alaska. And again, I did all I could to make your life safe and happy without ever interacting with you or your loved ones." He paused, an enigmatic shadow falling over his face. "When you died at the age of forty-two, surrounded by your mourning family, I cried again. Alone."

He closed his eyes, but not before she saw them shimmer with iridescent light. "I've watched you live each new life, I've watched you die, so many times. For centuries. A new life in New Zealand, followed by one in Poland. A new life in India. A new life in Switzerland. So many new lives, so many different places. I've never approached you in any of them, I never let you know of my existence. I never interfered in any way—except to make sure your everyday life was good and safe. As much as I wanted to have you look at me, smile at me, I couldn't allow myself to come to you. You'd loved me once, and it killed you. I couldn't forgive myself for that."

Tahlee struggled against the invisible pressure wrapping around her chest. Her head roared. Her mind flung up ghost images from lives she didn't remember, even as she knew—*knew*—those images were from her past lives.

Mouth dry, eyes burning, she dragged in a deep breath. Or tried to. Her throat didn't want to work. "How many times—"

He shook his head. "I'm not going to tell you."

"And you stayed away from me every time?"

"Yes."

"Until this life? Until I came back as...as me? Tahlee?"

His nostril flared.

"Why this time? Why didn't you stay..."

She couldn't say *away*. The word refused to form on her lips. Instead, she stared at him.

"You were never meant to see me in that pub," he said. The sorrow in his smile tore at her heart. "I'd let you go, you see. From my heart. I had to. For my own sanity. An insane djinn is a threat to *all* life...so I'd let you go. Somewhere around your eighth reincarnation. I made sure you were safe and happy in every reincarnation, but with every new life, I stepped back further." A hollow laugh fell from him and he rolled his eyes, rubbing at the back of his neck again. "I'd even convinced myself there would come a day when I'd realize I didn't know who you'd come back as... didn't recognize you. That you didn't mean anything to me anymore."

"So what happened?" Hell, how was she even breathing, let alone speaking?

He looked at her again. "I didn't move fast enough in the crowded pub. I never planned for you to bump into me. Please believe that, Hope. It was always for the best you never saw me, met me. But that night...I just wanted to watch you smiling and laughing, for as long as I could. And then you bumped into me, and looked at me, and I was lost. And despite knowing what could happen if I stayed with you, despite the consequences that could occur, I couldn't walk away from you again. I *couldn't*."

"What consequences?" Had all the air in the room vanished? Was that why it was so difficult to draw breath? "What would happen if you stayed with me, James?"

His Adam's apple bobbed as he swallowed. "Syrin's curse. The one he placed on me with his last breath. It—"

He stopped, eyes flaring to white. Tension coiled his muscles as his hands balled to fists. His glowing stare snapped to the bedroom door. "Stay here," he ordered without looking at her. "Don't—"

A man burst into the room, the same man Tahlee had met in the Guarded Souls office, his attention fixed solely on James. "We've got a problem, Jimmy Boy. The detective who took Ms. Hope's statement has disappeared. So has his wife—and Nathanial says their existence have been erased from not only the temporal, but the ethereal plane."

Tahlee's stomach clenched. The what? And the what?

James's jaw knotted. "Shite, that's not good. *Seriously* not good. But Kitt, Hope's safe here. This is the safest farking house on the planet, and she's with me. So why—"

Kitt shook his head, flicked Tahlee a quick look, and then frowned at James. "Someone using dark magic has started assaulting the Guarded Souls shielding wards. Specifically, the one concealing *your* existence. Nim thinks it's a sorcerer. A powerful one. And no matter what she does, she can't locate him."

James sucked in a breath. His eyes flared white again. "Farking bastard," he whispered.

And then, with a single click of his fingers, he became transparent.

7

Heart smashing into his throat, Philips drew a slow breath, tight triumph flowing through his veins as a man materialized in front of him.

The djinn.

Finally. After twenty minutes of nothing, he'd begun to think his summoning spell had failed.

Eyes glowing with white magic, the djinn flashed him a grin. "Ah, you. Gotta say, I thought you'd be taller."

Philips blinked. And then sneered. "Enough. You're mine now."

The djinn laughed. *Laughed*. As if the statement of fact was hilarious. "Oh shite, no. I just thought it was time we met."

A cold beat thumped in Philips's temples. His heart joined in. He cast a quick glance toward the smoldering, blood-soaked goat bones, scattered entrails, and melted wax at his feet before narrowing his eyes at Hastin. "My summoning spell worked. You're here."

Another grin. Another white flash of magic in pupil-less eyes. "Am I?"

"Yes. You are. Now come *to me.*" Philips raised his hand, palm up, fingers splayed, and then snapped his fist closed, yanking the djinn's energy forward,

Hastin didn't move.

Ice flooded Philips's veins. Fist to his gut, he stared at the djinn.

"Told you I wasn't here."

"How?" Lowering his hand, Philips rubbed his fingertips together. The residual stench of the summoning spell still hung on the air. The coppery taint of blood still slicked the back of his throat. "I summoned you."

Hastin laughed again. "Let's think this through, shall we? I'll help you out, given you're clearly not that bright." He tapped his chest with his index finger. "Djinn." Pointed at the floor with the same finger. "Mankind's realm." His grin returned, cold and scathing. It sent a shard of trepidation into Philips's gut. "If I'm already *in* this realm—and the fact you've been trying to discover information about me says you know I *am*—that means I've already been summoned here by another sorcerer, doesn't it? One smarter than you, it seems. So that means *you* can't summon me. Following?"

The unease in Philips's gut morphed into dark anger. "I am the most powerful sorcerer on Earth! I've destroyed my rivals and absorbed their power—*and* their memories. I would know if someone else brought you here from your realm."

"Blah blah blah." Hastin flapped his fingers together like a duck's bill and rolled his eyes. "I see your ego compensates for your height." He raked a slow gaze over Philips. "I mean, you really *are* short, aren't you? I'm talking Danny DeVito short."

"*Enough!*" Philips blasted a hot wall of raw energy at the djinn.

Hastin raised his eyebrows and looked about himself. "Well, that was...impotent."

Hate and rage bleeding together, Philips glared at him. "Why are you here then? *How* are you here?"

White eyes shimmered brighter. "You really don't know much about djinn, do you? I'm surprised I didn't find you rubbing on a lamp or something. A djinn only has to think about something to either get it, or go to it. As for the why?" A dark chuckle filled the space between them. "To let *you* know that *I* know what you've done. What you're trying to do. And to tell you to count your days."

A heavy rock dropped in Philips's stomach. What *did* the djinn know? How much? Did he know how many people Philips had terminated and destroyed guiding Rourke to his current political glory? Did he know how many natural laws he'd broken, how much dark magic he'd wrought, getting Rourke to where he was now—two elections away from being the so-called Leader of the Free World?

Did the djinn know he'd given the woman currently blackmailing the politician over his illegitimate baby a disease...one that mimicked bone cancer but was so much worse?

It was doubtful—but not impossible. The power of a djinn was mysterious, especially a djinn with an unknown master.

He needed to fix this. He'd locate that unknown master later, but for now...

Smoothing his hand over his head, he stretched his lips into a flattering smile. A cajoling smile. The one he used to get what he wanted on those rare occasions when he wasn't able to use sorcery. "I'll make you a deal. All I really want is the reporter. That's all. I have no *real* interest in you. More," he waved his hand around in a little circle, as if searching for a word, "professional curiosity, is all. Just give me the woman, and I'll pretend I never knew you existed. I'll forget all about you. We can forget about each other. From what I've seen of the hate-filled articles she writes, I'll be doing the human world a favor."

Hastin's nostrils flared. For a second, the very blood in Philips's veins seemed to turn to ice.

And then Hastin smiled. "You make an interesting argument...but I'm going to go with 'fuck you'."

The ice in Philips's veins grew colder. Brittle.

"Forget about me?" Hastin went on, voice relaxed. Jovial. Like an amused adult talking to a child. "Ha. You never *knew* me. You can't summon a djinn you don't know. Maybe you need to brush up on your djinn lore. Tell me, what name *did* you chant in your 'summoning' spell? Was it Hastin?"

Philips ground his teeth, even as the blood in his veins now flowed hot with humiliation and fresh anger.

The djinn snorted. "Thought so. And here I was, assuming you were a danger."

"I will fucking *own* you, djinn!" Philips screamed. "And when I do—"

"There's no mercy heading your way," Hastin cut him off, as calm and relaxed as before. "Only punishment and judgement. And I'm not talking about the human kind."

Jaw aching, Philips stepped forward. "I *will* find her. And I will locate the sorcerer who summoned you and gorge on his knowledge, and then you'll be *mine*, and I will order you to tear her apart limb from limb! Mark me."

Hastin threw back his head, his laugh rising to the ceiling. "Okay, maybe I *will* let you live. You're funny."

"*Enough!*" Philips roared. He flung out his hands, hurling anything he could snare with invisible energy at the djinn.

Each object—bones, candles, iron shackles, Mrs. Taylor's dismembered head—passed straight through Hastin's form.

The djinn's eyes flared again, and he seemed to grow bigger. Loomed larger. "How the mighty has fallen." His voice stabbed into Philips's ears. "A child's party magician would be more of a threat than you, *sorcerer.*"

Sorcerer...

Philips stiffened.

Rose, sorcerer...

The words sheared through his mind, bringing with them a fresh wave of the memories that had assaulted him earlier.

Yes, *memories.* That's what the vision had been, memories. *His* memories.

His!

But who was he then?

...killed Rose, sorcerer...

He stared at Hastin, branding every inch of the djinn's visage into his brain.

...killed Rose, sorcerer...

The djinn's voice from the memory screamed—*You killed Rose, sorcerer*—digging at something deeply buried in Philips's past, something important, something...powerful.

What *was* it? What...

Name. The djinn's name. It's there. You know it. You—

"We're coming for you, sorcerer." Thick purple smoke swirled around Hastin, even as his form became translucent. "And you will suffer for *everything* you've ever done."

"I know you," Philips snarled, inching closer to Hastin's fading image.

Hastin's eyes erupted with blinding-white light. So bright, Philips threw up a shielding arm and cried out.

"You know fuck-all, Syrin," the djinn's voice whispered from the white light. "You never did."

And then, the white vanished.

Philips lowered his arm, eyes squinting against an expected onslaught of brightness.

It didn't come. Nothing did. No sound. No movement. Nothing.

Gone.

Pivoting slowly, he took in his work room through foggy vision.

The djinn was gone.

"Fuck!"

Rage cracked through him, and he snatched up Mrs. Taylor's head and slammed it back to the floor. What *was* the fucking djinn prick's name? His true name? Without the power of Hastin's true name, Philips could do nothing against or to him.

Scrunching his face, red flashes still blooming on his retinas from the djinn's white light, he searched through his mind. Dug into the deepest pits of his memory.

The djinn's name was there somewhere. He just needed to find...

A hot prickle crawled over his flesh and he opened his eyes, a slow smile stretching his lips.

"Syrin." Not the djinn's name. The very bones in his body told him that. But an important name. A name the djinn had foolishly, arrogantly, uttered in contempt.

Syrin.

A name to hook a recollection spell on.

"Thank you, Hastin," he murmured, striding across his workroom to a massive oak bookshelf.

His smile stretched wider as he opened a small and ornate bronze chest on the middle shelf.

A needle-sharp dagger lay nestled on a small black velvet pillow. Carved from the rib of the virgin high priestess of Moneta, the Roman goddess of memory, the dagger had been lost to time for hundreds of years until a collector of rare iniquities gloated about possessing it to Philips one night in a seedy bar.

The collector didn't survive the night. His collection had found a new home with Philips.

Closing his eyes, Philips whispered the complicated Latin incantation required to touch the dagger. Without the ancient words, he'd forget everything—including how to breathe—the second his skin touched the bleached bone. With the words, however...

A hot ripple passed through him. His dick hardened.

Opening his eyes, he retrieved the dagger, held it aloft, admiring its ageless, powerful beauty, and then pressed its point to the middle of his left temple.

"Recall Syrin," he whispered.

And pushed the dagger's tip into his flesh.

THAT WAS STUPID.

It was.

Why had he done that?

Retracting his projection back into his body, he

dragged his hands through his hair. Provoking Syrin was idiotic.

He's not Syrin.

The denial scraped at him and he let out a harsh breath.

Deny it all he liked, the truth had slammed into him the second he'd materialized in the sorcerer's presence. Syrin—Rose's father—walked the earth again. Reincarnated and clueless, yes. But alive all the same.

And powerful.

The sorcerer's force had almost torn him apart. When Syrin—

No, in this life, he was Philips. Doug Philips. Ha, hardly a fearsome name.

When *Philips* had attempted to snare James's energy, enslave him with a command, James had almost capitulated.

It was only the fact Philips didn't know the name Barqan that had allowed James to resist him.

But his force...the power in his magic...

James clawed at his scalp again.

Fark, he'd just provoked Syrin. The sorcerer who'd summoned him and trapped him here in mankind's realm. Who still had the power to control him. Not only provoked him, but used his name. How could he have done *that*? A slip of the tongue was one thing, but giving Philips any kind of knowledge of who he once was...

Fark, he'd lost control.

And why? Because Philips had dared threaten Tahlee. But of course, he *would*. The whole reason Tahlee was under the protection of Guarded Soul was because she'd heard him —Philips—threatening the life of another unknown woman.

Philips had no clue of Tahlee's relationship to James. Of course he'd want to get his hands on her; what she'd overheard could destroy him, and most likely Maximillian Rourke, as well.

Stupid. Idiotic.

Dangerous.

"James?"

Tahlee's soft voice made him drop his hands. He lifted his head and turned to face her.

Worry ate up her face, and the urge to translocate completely to Philips and rip his black heart out surged through him. If it wasn't for the bastard sorcerer, she wouldn't be in this state.

If it wasn't for Syrin, you never would have met her.

His chest tightened. As true at that was, he couldn't find any sympathy for the sorcerer.

The fact Philips was Syrin reincarnated also meant James couldn't actually cause him any harm. Not unless the sorcerer made a foolish wish. In that regard, the bastard had James by the balls, whether he knew it or not.

No matter how much James wanted to erase Syrin's reincarnated arse from existence, he couldn't.

"Where did you go, James?" Tahlee asked, voice calm. Her reporter's voice. He'd heard it many times; the tone she used to process shit she didn't like at all.

James flicked Kitt—standing silently beside her—a quick look.

The wolf shifter regarded him, expression wary. Tension rolled from him, an animalistic aggression.

Kitt would gut Philips in a heartbeat if James asked him to. Shift into his dire wolf form and disembowel him.

James had seen Kitt deal with a murderous threat in just such a way before. A Guarded Souls job that turned deadly, when everyone who worked there was almost killed. The wolf shifter didn't fuck about when it came to those he cared for being threatened. All James would have to do is ask...

Any of the team would move on the sorcerer.

But if Philips discovered who he was, who he'd once been in a past life, he'd have the power to force James to eliminate every Guarded Souls team member with a single wish.

If Philips connected his past life with James, no one was safe.

"Jimmy Boy?" Kitt's low voice rumbled through the stretching silence. "Do I need to call Kade? Nim?"

"No." James shook his head. "I've dealt...I'm dealing with Philips."

"Philips?" Tahlee's eyes narrowed. "Who's Philips?"

"The man you overheard in the toilet at the art gallery. He won't—"

"You called whoever you were talking to Syrin," she said. "Not Philips."

He studied her, waiting for the proverbial shoe to drop.

A frown dipped her eyebrows, and she narrowed her stare at him. "Syrin. That's the name of my father, isn't it? I mean, the name of my father when I was Rose."

And there it is

Kitt's eyebrows shot up. "Syrin is the sorcerer who brought James to this realm over a thousand years ago. What do you mean, he's your father? What do you mean, *when you were Rose*?" He swung his attention back to James. "Rose is the human you fell in love with, right? How can Tahlee be Rose? What the ever-loving fuck is going on?"

"It's all good, Rover."

Kitt's amber eyes flared gold. "Don't *Rover* me, genie. What aren't you telling us?"

"What the hell?" Tahlee gasped, stare locked on Kitt..

James bit back a groan. If he didn't calm Kitt's overprotective agitation, she'd witness the rather jarring—to a human, at least—transformation of a man into a massive wolf. She didn't need that. Not at the moment. It would probably be the sanity-shattering icing on the cake, given the last twenty-four hours she'd endured.

So, Tahlee...genies are real, you're the reincarnated soul of a woman from over a thousand years ago, your father back then was a murderous sorcerer—and he, too, has been resurrected. Oh hey, he wants you dead...and by the way, good ol' Kitt here can shift into the form of a dire wolf whenever he damn well pleases. Cool, huh?

Yeah, she didn't need that. Which meant he had to defuse Kitt. Now.

"Kitt," he said, meeting the wolf-shifter's glowing eyes. "It's okay. We're all okay. Honestly." Bit of a stretch there. "What we all need now is a cup of tea." He pointed a finger at Tahlee, letting a relaxed grin play with his lips. "You'd like a cup of tea, wouldn't you, Hope?"

She looked at him like he'd grown an extra head.

He grinned wider. "I'd like a cup of tea." He returned his focus to Kitt. "And I know *you're* partial to a good Darjeeling, Rover, because the Darjeeling teabags I keep in the staff kitchen go missing almost every week, and I know you're the culprit."

Kitt's eyes flickered back to amber. The knot in his jaw loosened. "Jim, you need to tell me what's—"

"I will, Rover." Was it the use of Kitt's nickname or the resignation in his voice? Whatever it was, the tension left Kitt and he frowned at James. Giving the wolf shifter a sheepish smile, James chuckled. "I promise. Over a cup of tea. I think we all need it."

Kitt's broad chest swelled with a deep, slow breath. "Okay." He gave Tahlee a quick glance. "I'll go make it. Let you two finish up whatever it was you were doing before I barged in."

He hurried from the bedroom without another word.

"Shoulda just conjured up a stick and threw it," James murmured.

"What the hell is going on, James?" Tahlee's fingers wrapped around his wrist and he turned back to her. Yep, the journalist was back. But a shadow of uncertainty darkened her eyes. "No flippant charm, no sheepish sidestepping. I want simple answers. Please?"

Her voice cracked on the plea and before he could stop himself, he cupped her face in his hands and brushed a soft kiss over her lips.

His Rose, his Tahlee. His Hope.

Hope for an existence he'd never thought he'd have. Hope for a love he knew he could never accept.

His Hope.

She sighed into the kiss, and sighed again when he broke it.

Tears shone in her eyes as she stared up at him. "Talk to me, my love." She pressed her palms to his chest and gave his shirtfront a gentle tug. "I don't care about Syrin, or who I used to be. All I want to know right now is why you left me three years ago. I need you to explain that to me. I need to understand that first."

Chest tight, he closed his eyes.

"Please," she whispered.

Opening his eyes, he brushed his thumb over her bottom lip, and then took a step backward. "The curse

Syrin placed on me with his last breath..." He let out a ragged breath of his own, and then chuckled at the bleak irony of it. "It devastated him, you see. Having his beloved daughter fall in love with a djinn was bad enough—a creature far more powerful than he was or could ever be, but to have a djinn love her in return? Offer her a life away from his oppressive control, his possessive, unnatural affection. That infuriated him. Destroyed him. On an emotional level. Tore his selfish, perverse heart apart. His daughter belonged to him. No other male—whether human or magical being—could have her. So he cursed me to experience his pain. If I ever fell in love again, and gave voice to that love, admitted it to another, my *djinn's* heart—the source of my magic and immortality—would be forfeit. I would become mortal...and eventually die."

Tahlee's eyes widened.

"And the second, the very second you told me you loved me in that restaurant in Wimbledon, I felt the words form on my lips, the words to tell you I loved you in return —and I ran."

She stared at him.

"That's why I left you," he finished. "Because without my djinn's heart, I am nothing."

More importantly, if he wasn't a djinn, he couldn't do what needed to be done if she was in danger. Not just in her Tahlee reincarnation, but in all those to follow.

An unreadable frown dipped her forehead. She narrowed her eyes at him. "What does that mean? You'd stop being a djinn and become human?"

"I think so."

"So you'd die? Straight away? Or would you live like a normal human?"

"I don't know. Maybe. I've only known of two djinn

who've lost their hearts in mankind's realm. Neither returned to the djinn realm."

"They suffered?"

His chest tightened. "There are rumors, some absurd. Some believe they died of old age."

"Old age."

He nodded. Old, impotent age. Incapable of anything except being...ineffective.

Her frown faded and she shook her head. "So I *was* wrong, after all."

"When?"

Her eyes closed for a second as she rubbed a hand over her face, and then she met his stare again. "When we first came face to face back at in the Guarded Souls office. You said you left me without a word because you were a coward, and I said you were a lot of things...but not a coward."

The memory of their confrontation sank into James's chest. The sting in her words followed.

"I would have surrendered everything I knew for us, James," she said. "I would have changed everything for us. But...but you..." She shook her head. "Did you even contemplate it? Or even think about talking to me? Or did you just run because that was the easiest option?"

"Tahlee." Her name fell from him on a whisper. "That's not... It's not what you think."

"Perhaps I was wrong about you, James." Disappointment shone in her eyes. Rivaled only by pain. "Maybe you *are* a coward."

Wish it away, Jimmy Boy. Wish it—

BARQAN! a cold, triumphant voice boomed in his head.

A familiar voice.

Ice flooded through him, at the very second every molecule in his ethereal body began to vibrate.

"Fark," he breathed, gaze holding Tahlee's. "He's remembered my name. He's remembered my—"

BARQAN, BY YOUR NAME, I SUMMON AND ENSLAVE YOU, Syrin finished, tearing James's existence apart.

The safe house vanished. Everything vanished. No light no sound, no darkness. Nothing layered over nothing as he flung through Actuality, incapable of denying the summons of the sorcerer who'd first pulled him from his realm.

Incapable of doing anything until, a heartbeat later, he materialized into the very room in which he'd projected himself a few short minutes ago.

"Welcome back, djinn." With a nasty smile, Philips flicked the fresh goat's blood and entrails dripping from his fingers into James's face. "Told you that you'd be mine."

James balled his fists. "You've made a mistake, Syrin. You will suffer for—"

"*Kneel*, djinn," Philips snarled, slamming his open hands in a downward direction.

James crumpled to his knees.

Incapable of doing anything else.

Enslaved and controlled, once again, by the most malicious sorcerer he'd ever encountered.

TAHLEE BOLTED FOR THE KITCHEN, the sheer terror in James's face as he disappeared before her eyes lashing at her sanity.

He had him.

Syrin had him.

What does that even mean?

She had no clue. Except for what the horror in James's eyes told her.

It was bad. Worse than bad.

Oh God, James.

"Kitt!" she yelled, sprinting into the kitchen. "He's got James!"

Kitt spun from the counter, eyes glowing gold, a growl rumbling deep in his chest.

She skidded to a halt, her bare heels slipping on the cool tiles, her heart smashing into her throat. "Kitt, it's me!" she yelped. "Tahlee. James's Tahlee."

James's Tahlee.

The gold light evaporated and, staring at her with human eyes again, he took a step closer. "*Who's* got James?"

"I think...I think Syrin."

He growled again. Jesus, what a scary flipping sound. "What do you mean, Syrin?"

He didn't wait for an answer. Instead, he ran from the kitchen. "Oi, Jimmy Boy!" he yelled.

Tahlee ran after him. Ran *into* him when he stopped just inside the bedroom.

"He was here," she said, rubbing at her knee. Better to concentrate on the small ache from running into a six-foot-plus mountain of a man than the angry words she'd said to James...and the dread on his face when he'd vanished a few seconds after.

It's not what you think...

His voice, low and racked with pain.

He's remembered my name. He's remembered my—

His last words. Full of horror.

A sick weight rolled in her stomach. "We need to save him!"

Kitt held up his hand. His back swelled with a deep, slow breath. "I can't detect anything." Worry shone in his eyes as he flicked her a quick glance over his shoulder. "What happened?"

The weight in her stomach doubled. Her blood roared in her ears. "We were talking. And then fear filled his face and—"

"Fear?" Kitt's eyebrows rose. "I've never seen James afraid in all the time I've known him."

"He was scared. *Terrified*. And he said, 'He's remembered my name. He's remembered my—' And then he just disappeared." She clicked her fingers. "Like that."

Kitt winced.

"I think it's Syrin," she went on. Panic gnawed at her. Took great, hungry bites out of her. "Somehow, Philips—the man I overheard—is also Syrin, the sorcerer who brought James into this world. I think he's somehow summoned him again, using his name, his *real* name, Barqan. And now we have to save him! We have to save James! I have to find him!" She pressed her palm to her mouth. Anything to stop the bitter sob about to burst from her.

Perhaps I was wrong about you, James.

Her last words to him—spoken in hurt, anger—scraped at her soul. *Maybe you are a coward.*

"I have to save him," she whispered into her hand.

"Fuck." Kitt raked a hand through his thick hair. "Nim doesn't know where this sorcerer is. She tried to locate him and failed."

Tahlee balled her fists. She didn't know who Nim was,

and she didn't care. If Nim couldn't help find James, she wasn't worth wondering about.

Scrunching up her face, she racked her brain. There had to be *something* that would help. Something that would give her a place to start.

"Philips," she muttered, opening her eyes. "He works for Maximillian Rourke, right? There has to be some way of finding information about those who work for Rourke —their local offices, their private home address. Something like that. We know who Philips is, just not where to find him."

And how long will that take? What will Syrin, Philips, your father...what will the sorcerer bastard do to James while you're doing that?

What else could she do? She wasn't a genie. Or magical. She couldn't just fold her arms and blink and get what she wanted. If she could do that, she would have blinked James back three years ago.

"Find Philips, find James. That's the answer," she said, pointing at Kitt. "I need a laptop. Surely there's one—"

The bedroom vanished, replaced by a large, immaculate room with a wide mahogany desk, a framed, tattered American flag, and a curtained window.

"—here," she whispered.

Where?

Her stomach dropped. Her breath turned to stone in her throat. She gaped at the strange room, her lips and fingertips tingling as if every drop of blood in her body had suddenly been sucked from her veins and injected back in again. Violently.

What the—

"Tahlee!" James's voice called behind her. "I'm—"

"Silence!" a male voice, a *familiar* male voice, snarled as she spun around.

James kneeled a few feet away. What looked like molten ropes with ends that evaporated into thin air bound his wrists, stretching his arms out wide to either side of his body.

"Tahlee," James breathed, stare locked on her.

"And here she is." A short man ambled into her line of sight. "The perfect first wish."

The short man.

The man from the restroom.

Philips.

Syrin.

"Hello, Ms. Hope," he said, raking a slow gaze over her. "Glad you could join us."

She launched herself at him, ready to draw blood, to break bones. Ready to hurt him, *really* hurt him, for what he'd done to James.

Without hesitation, she ran at him. She knew how to fight. Was scrappy at it. Fuck fighting fair.

And screamed as an invisible force flung her sideways.

"No!" James's roar rent the air a second before she slammed into the wall.

Pain lashed through her shoulder, her neck, her hip.

She dropped to the floor, catching herself before she could crumple completely.

Wobbling on her feet, she pressed a hand to the wall and glared over at Philips. "I take it you're responsible for me being here?"

He smiled, extending his hand toward where James stood immobilized by the oozing, dripping binds. "When you have a djinn in your pocket..."

"Clearly there's plenty of room in your trousers, in that

case." She flicked a look at his groin. "If you can fit a whole djinn in your pocket."

"Tahlee," James groaned. "Don't."

Philips's lip curled in a sneer. "Fucking little cunt."

"Hey!" James roared.

Philips flinched, darting his stare to where James fought against the molten bonds.

"You hurt her again," James said, eyes glowing white, the veins on his neck popping, "and—"

"And what?" Philips sneered. "*I* control *you*, djinn. Remember? *I* summoned *you*."

James's eyes flared brighter. "Not forever. The covenant is *never* endless."

Philips sucked in a sharp breath and jerked his gaze back to Tahlee.

"And a djinn never forgets," James finished, a world of promised pain in the words.

She narrowed her eyes at Philips. How could this...this *disgusting* man be her father in a former life? Looking at him made her sick. Furious.

Violent.

"So, we're at an impasse," she said. "You hurt me now, James will one day kill you." She arched an eyebrow. "I may be new to this whole sorcerer/djinn power dynamic, but I'm pretty certain he's got you over a barrel."

Contempt twisted Philips's face into a hideous, angry mask. "You talk too much, bitch."

He raised his hands, fingers bending and wriggling, and muttered something under his breath.

Tahlee frowned. What the hell was—

"No!" James roared, a second before something thick and heavy snaked around her face, covering her mouth.

What the—

She clawed at it, fingers scrabbling over the mass of thin, cool strands of...of...

Oh God, her hair!

He'd gagged her with her own hair.

Her fingers tore at the strands, but with every tiny snap, the thick rope of hair wrapped around her head tighter.

Silencing her.

"Stop it!" James yelled, veins bulging in his neck, his stare locked on her.

"Shush, djinn," Philips said haughtily.

The molten bands binding James glowed brighter, light dripping from them in fat beads that hissed and burned when they hit the floor.

"Let her go!" James shouted, fighting against them, fists clenched tight, eyes white.

Philips laughed, fingers bending and jerking in a hypnotic rhythm as he slowly walked toward Tahlee.

She shook her head and took a step away, still clawing at her hair.

No. No no no!

"Now," Philips said, "what can I do with you?"

Tahlee swallowed. Pain seared through her jaw. Each frantic breath she sucked in through her nose burned her nostrils.

"I will make you suffer, sorcerer," James growled.

"Oh, I'm not going to *hurt* her." Philips threw over his shoulder, studying Tahlee as he drew closer.

Closer.

She threw herself at him again. Gagged by her hair or not, she could still—

He waved his hand, as if shooing away a fly, and she smashed backward into the wall. Pinned there by an invisible force.

"Prick," she tried to shout through her hair, the word nothing but a muffled mumbled.

"Stop!" James bellowed.

Philips raked a slow inspection over her. "What's so special about this...female?" He stopped directly in front of her, lip curling. "I've seen hotter."

"You fucking bastard," Tahlee raged into her hair.

Philips chortled. "Although I do admire her spirit. I suspect she'd rip my throat out if I let her."

He looked back at James. "Is it just the paid bodyguard thing?"

James glared at him, fists bunching tighter, muscles bulging as he struggled against his bonds.

"Surprising work for a djinn, I must admit," Philips went on. "Unless you're incapable of using your full djinn power since I'd trapped you here in my former life. Is that how it goes? You had to get a job?"

Tahlee grew still. Her stomach churned. How much did Philips remember about his existence as Syrin? Did he know how Syrin had died? Or why?

He didn't know who *she* was to Syrin. Not with the way he was talking about her...but did he know about Rose and Barqan?

"You've been stuck here in mankind's realm for a long time. Long enough to form relationships, it seems." Eyes narrowing, Philips slid his stare back to her. "Which means this bitch may not be just a client you've been paid to protect."

James's eyes flared white.

Philips ran another slow gaze over her. "How would you feel if I fucked her? It's almost poetic, isn't it. You fucked my daughter, the only living thing I ever loved. You sank your unnatural djinn dick in her, you took what was *mine*, so I think it's only just I take what *you* clearly believe is yours. An eye for an eye, yes? Or should that be, a cunt for a cunt?"

"*Don't you touch her!*" James roared.

Tahlee's throat slammed shut. Her stomach rolled. She writhed against the wall, her hair tightening around her face.

Philips tapped his finger against his lips. "What if I wish for her to become my sexual slave? Or better yet," he clicked his fingers and turned back to James, "I could wish for her to fall in love with me. Something tells me that would devastate you, djinn. And there's no way you could twist that wish to harm me. Not without harming *her*." He chortled again, the sound smug. Hateful. "And once she's mine, I control you even more."

James's nostrils flared. His stare didn't leave Philips. The air around him seemed to darken, as if the particles themselves were bruised.

Philips nodded, swinging back to face Tahlee. "Yes, I like that idea. We could have some fun with it. And by we, I mean me, of course. You, djinn, would just have to watch. But I guess, after all these centuries, you're used to being impotent, aren't you?" He let out another smug snort. "And now you're back under the control of your summoning master. Well, be sure in the knowledge I will be putting that power of yours to *very* good use. We'll start with the bitch here sucking my cock, and then move onto... *Hmmm*, perhaps *me* becoming president instead of that moron, Rourke. And finish off with—"

"You're a monumentally dumb individual in this life, Syrin," James said.

Tahlee blinked, not just at the insult, but at how calm he sounded all of a sudden. How amused.

Philips's mouth fell open before he snapped it shut. "Be careful, djinn."

James pulled a contemplative face, the tension flowing from his body, his white eyes trained on Philips. "Y'know what? I'm not going to call you that—Syrin. You're not worthy of the name. Syrin was a powerful, intelligent sorcerer. Narcissistic, yes, but clever. He had style. Poise. You, *Doug*, are just a petty little wannabe. Control a djinn? Ha. You truly know nothing about the sorcerer/djinn dynamic, let alone how to reap the benefits of it."

A crack shattered the air. The windows rattled. The molten bands keeping James on his knees ignited.

Philips stalked toward him, each step making the room shudder. "I am the most powerful sorcerer alive, djinn. You are nothing but my *slave*! As all djinn truly are. Slaves to their sole purpose—to grant wishes. I'm in control of you. While our covenant stands, I *rule* you. You can't refuse me. You may try to twist my words, but as long as the bitch over there *loves* me," he groaned the word, turning it into a mocking threat, "you don't ever get to win!"

James nodded, as if agreeing...and then shook his head with a laugh. "I really think you've been watching too many Disney movies."

Tahlee's stomach knotted. What was he doing?

Philips stopped in front of him, driving a finger up under his chin. "Be wary of your words, djinn."

"In the immortal words of one Bartholomew J. Simpson," James said. "Eat my shorts."

The air around the lower half of his body glowed purple for a split second, and then a pair of baggy cargo shorts replaced the faded jeans he'd been wearing.

"What?" Philips reeled back.

James flicked his legs a quick look. "Sorry. Wrong kind."

The purple light—like glowing mist—swirled over his legs again, vanishing to reveal a comically plain pair of blue shorts, the kind worn by a cartoon ten-year-old boy. "That's better."

Tahlee laughed against the gag of her hair.

"How?" Philips stuttered, the air around him crackling.

James's eyes burned whiter. "As I said, Doug, you're a lowly, incompetent sorcerer. The power of a djinn is beyond you. You might *think* you control me, but my djinn power is mine alone. You will *never* be able to wield it." His fists bunched. "So don't fucking try."

Another crack filled the room. Philips stood motionless, fear in his face, stare locked on James.

Tahlee's heart slammed into her tight throat. What was James doing? What was—

In a blur, Philips snagged a fistful of James's hair and yanked his head back.

"Stop it," Tahlee tried to shout.

"Then let's amend that, shall we?" Philips sneered, bending over until his face hung barely an inch from James's.

"*No!*" Tahlee screamed into her hair, even as it wrapped unbearably tight around her head.

Philips flicked a hand at her without taking his stare from James, and her hair suddenly covered her whole face.

No. No no!

She bucked against the invisible force pinning her to the wall, incapable of clawing her hair from her eyes, her nose.

Oh God!

"What are you saying, Doug?" James asked, voice low,

cold. "Think about what you're doing. Don't be foolish. Don't—"

"I wish to absorb your djinn powers, Barqan," Philips stated, each word louder that the last. "Make them mine now!"

Tahlee's stomach sank.

"I was really *wishing* you'd say that," James whispered —a second before a deep boom resonated through the room and Tahlee's hair fell from her face.

She staggered sideways, rubbing her eyes, the sudden rush of air on her skin jarring even as sweet relief rushed through her.

"What?" Philips's shocked gasp snapped her attention to where he stood, gaping up at James as he slowly straightened to his feet in front of him.

Dark purple smoke swirled around James, and as she watched, he changed. Grew taller, broader. His hair whipped around his face, longer and darker in color. His eyes burned a white so bright, they defied description, almost bleaching out his features. His clothes shimmered, becoming an iridescent robe of the darkest purple that floated around his body as if it were a living thing, the edges undefined as it moved with the roiling smoke.

Philips stumbled backward, arm in front of his face, head shaking. "How is this possible?"

James grew. Dominated the room. Towered over the sorcerer.

No, not James.

The djinn her past self had loved over a thousand years ago.

Barqan.

"*This isn't possible!*" Philips screamed, gibbering up at the looming djinn. "I am your master! I—"

Another deafening boom echoed through the room...

And James stood there again, now in faded jeans and a "Yoda for President" T-shirt, a grin on his face.

James. The man *she* loved. The man she'd loved since the second she'd met him.

"Did you like the booms?" he asked, sliding his hands into his back pockets, green eyes dancing with playful mischief. "I thought they added a great vibe. Y'know, really emphasized the significance of the moment."

"Enough!" Philips screeched, thrusting his hands toward James. "Djinn, I command you to—"

"Zip it, Doug." James made a quick gesture and Philips's lips snapped shut. "You broke our covenant. When you wished for the impossible, you broke our covenant."

Philips shook his head frantically, fingers prying at his closed mouth.

"What?" James's grin turned icy. "You're trying to say something?" He *tsked-tsked*; a patient adult dealing with a problem child. "You really should have brushed up on your djinn knowledge before saying my name, Doug. If you had, you would have known making a wish that's impossible and lethal immediately destroys the covenant. And wishing to take *my* magic for your own is pretty farking impossible. And just as lethal. To me. And a djinn cannot grant a wish that would result in their own demise. Ergo, you fucked up. Big time. "

A wave of something close to joy rushed through Tahlee, and a soft laughing breath fell from her before she could bite it back.

James flicked her a quick glance, and then smiled at Philips. "Syrin knew that. See? I told you that you were smarter back then."

Dropping his hands from his mouth, Philips hunched his shoulders, moving his fingers in front of his chest in small, jerky motions.

Every hair on Tahlee's body stood on end. "James!" she called, as the air seemed to be sucked out of her lungs. "He's trying to use his magic. He's—"

An invisible wave exploded from Philips, a blast of unseen force. It slammed into her, flinging her backward, just as James threw up his hands. A pillar of dark smoke lashed around her, halting her violent fall.

"Yield, Barqan," Philips's voice pummeled at her eardrums, "to *my* magic!"

The smoke vanished as the unseen force blasted outward again.

James lurched backward, pain etching his face. Eyes white once more, he threw back his head, his scream raw and tortured.

"No!" Tahlee yelled, running at Philips.

He swung an arm at her, fingers splayed, and an invisible hammer smashed her into another wall.

"Yield, Barqan," Philips repeated, hands thrust at James once again, "to *my* magic. *My* power."

James screamed again, spine bowing, arms flung wide.

The molten bands appeared again, lashing around his wrists, pulling his arms wide.

"Kneel, djinn!" Philips bellowed, driving his palms toward the floor. "Kneel!"

James's knees shook. The thick tendrils of purple smoke broiling around him shrank, eddied away.

"James!" Tahlee cried, fighting against the unseen forcing imprisoning her.

Do something. Help him.

How? How could she possibly overpower a sorcerer? She was just a human.

"*Kneel!*" Philips screeched.

"*NO!*" James roared, driving his arms down and across his torso with such otherworldly speed, the bands of burning magic around his wrists shattered.

Philips squealed, flailing backwards. "Stop! St—"

A column of smoke punched through the air, slamming into him. Another followed, and another. Driving him back, back, close to where Tahlee remained stuck, until he tumbled to the floor.

James stepped from the smoke, eyes white, expression calm. "I kneel for no one, Doug. Not anymore."

"You can't kill me," Philips snarled, one hand partially shielding his face. "I know that much. Even without a treaty, a djinn can't kill the summoning sorcerer. And if I make no wishes, there's nothing you can do to me."

"A little knowledge is a dangerous thing," James said, striding toward him.

"I know it's true!" Philips shot back, scrambling to his feet. "You do as well."

Still pinned to the wall, Tahlee's blood ran cold at the dark look on James's face. His expression said it all. It *was* true.

Philips sneered, back pressed to the wall beside her, stare locked on James. "I *will* control you, djinn. And when I do, I will make you destroy everything, *everyone* your miscreant's heart holds dear—starting with the bitch right here. She'll wish she never knew you!"

Wish.

She will wish...

"No," James growled. The air cracked. The room shook. The smoke billowed.

And as it did, Philips laughed. "There's nothing you can do, djinn. *I* have the power." He lashed out a hand, lightning arcing into the air as he grabbed Tahlee's wrist in a brutal grip. "And I'm going to enjoy using it against the cunt you seem to love so—"

"...you'll wish you'd never spoken to the djinn, Rose. You're mine. When I'm finished, you will curse its name and reject it for the abomination it is!" The switch cut into her bare back, tearing at her skin. "I am your father, Rose. You obey my *wishes! You belong to me!" The switch slashed at the back of her neck, flaying her flesh. "Do you hear me?" The switch tore at her hip, her breast. "It will not have you. I'll destroy your heart before I'll allow you to give it to the djinn." Pain sheared through her as the switch cut into her thighs, her stomach. "Your cunt is mine and I'll destroy anyone or anything that takes what's..."*

Tahlee gasped, head spinning, the sudden memory— Rose's memory—like a tsunami of hate and fear and misery crashing over her.

"Oh my God!" she shouted, rage incinerating everything inside her as she glared at Philips. "You were the *worst* fucking father ever! You *are* the worst fucking father!"

Philips snapped his stare to her. "What?"

"*I'm* Rose!"

"Tahlee, no!" James shouted.

Philips gaped at her, eyes wide. "*Rose*?" he whispered. Confusion etched his face, dissolving into stunned recognition, and he let out a choked groan. "My beloved Rose?"

A cold grin stretched her lips even as her stomach lurched at the feverish desire igniting in his eyes. "Yep. Rose. Reincarnated. Surprise, fuckwit."

Wish. She will wish...

Fury distorting his face, his grip on her wrist tightened. "I *remember*! I remember *everything*. *You* chose the djinn over me, you filthy, monster-fucking slut. I remember it all now. You were mine; only mine, and you chose *it* over your own flesh and blood. You deserved to die back then, just as you deserve to die now!"

"You know what, Doug?" she said, leaning toward him as much as she could, stare locked on his. "I *wish* for you to go to Hell."

The sound of James's swift intake of breath cracked the air.

She turned her head to look at him, just as—gaze fixed on hers—he whispered, "Done."

Deep in the bowels of the room, a shudder began. The windows rattled. Objects fell from the shelves, vibrated across the desk, shattering onto the floor.

"What..." Philips rasped, cowering away from her, eyes wide. "What did you do?"

The unseen force pinning her to the floor vanished, and she stumbled a step, righting herself even as the floor trembled beneath her feet.

"What's going on?" Philips howled, eyes darting all around the room.

Something cold and ancient shrieked from a place beyond Tahlee's comprehension. Her flesh crawled. Her breath caught in her throat.

She glanced at James.

Found Barqan instead, his expression unreadable, his eyes blazing white.

"*What have you done!?*" Philips screamed, lunging at her.

Tahlee flinched, bracing for impact—but he fell backward, as if shoved by an unseen hand.

Flailing to his feet again, he looked at Barqan. "Stop! Undo her wish. Undo—"

The air groaned and, with an ear-splintering rip, the floor ruptured, a black maw spewing foul mist and blood-curdling screams.

"No." Philips shook his head, bulging eyes fixed on the gaping wound. "No. *No!*"

The shriek came again, louder this time.

Tahlee shrank backward, and squealed as she bumped into something firm and warm.

"I've got you," James's voice whispered as strong arms wrapped around her. "You're safe."

She gaped up at him—James. Not Barqan. James. *Her* James.

Tahlee pushed herself closer to his body as she looked back at Philips.

Just as a vaporous black shadow oozed from the pit in the floor.

The very air froze. Another shriek tore at the silence, rising high until Philips began to whimper.

"No! I'm sorry, I'm sorry," he cried, shrinking against the wall.

The shadow hung poised on the edge of the hole for a moment, blackness broiling in blackness, consuming light, life, hope—and then it devoured the space between the maw and Philips, growing larger, taking shape. Thick, long arms, massive shoulders, a faceless head...

Tahlee pushed deeper into James's embrace, unable to look away even as her stomach churned and her mouth filled with sour fear.

And cold, dark elation.

"No!" Philips gibbered. "I didn't mean to... I don't belong down there! I'm not meant to go—"

The shadow reached out a nebulous hand and covered his face with blackness, eyeless head cocked to the side, as if waiting. Contemplating.

"No," Philips cried through the thick black mist. "Please! I'm sorry. I'm sorry. I'll change. I'll be better. I'm sorry. I'm—"

"*OURS*," a soulless voice boomed from the pit, a split second before the shadow shrieked, engulfed Philips's entire head with its vaporous hand, and dragged him, thrashing, flailing, into the gaping maw.

A thunderous crack rocked the room, reverberating through Tahlee's very soul...

And the hole vanished, as if it had never been there.

Silence filled the room, broken only by her ragged, shallow breaths.

Silence.

She stared at the pristine floor, heart thumping in her ears. A vice wrapped her chest. Her head spun.

"I did that," she whispered, shock turning her voice to a cracked rasp.

She'd killed a man. Oh God, she'd killed a man!

"No." James touched a finger to her chin, lifting her face to his. "*I* did that."

She swallowed. Frowned. Shook her head and looked at the floor again. Her brain replayed the moment over and over, Philips's pleas growing louder each time, the shadow growing darker, larger. "I wished him to Hell," she croaked. "I knew what I was doing." She looked back at James, her stomach clenching. "I *knew* what I was saying, and I said it anyway. I did it!"

"You made the wish, Hope," he said, brushing a thumb over her cheek. "But I didn't have to grant it. I *chose* to."

"Is...is he gone for good?"

James dipped his head in a small nod. "I'll check with Feath— Nathanial, the angel who works for Guarded Souls, to be sure, but usually when Hell claims a soul, there's no coming back."

A ghost of a memory of her life as Rose whispered through her mind, her father—Syrin—ranting about the filthy, poor villagers always wanting his help.

Another memory followed—Philips's words in the bathroom at the Getty, ordering a woman's tongue to be ripped out of her mouth.

"Good," she said quietly. "He belongs there."

"Yeah." James nodded again. "He—"

Raising onto her toes, she kissed him. She needed the warmth of his lips on hers, needed his strength, his touch, his passion to scour away the fear and rage of Philips's attack.

Needed it all, an assurance James was there, with her.

She tangled her hands in his hair and groaned as he scooped her harder to his body, his mouth and tongue moving with hers, meeting her hunger with his own.

They crumpled to the floor, lips never breaking, hands cupping faces, exploring backs, fisting in hair.

And then, with a low groan, he pulled away, his breath as choppy as hers.

Shaking, her fingers slipping over the back of his neck, she stared up into his eyes, so green, so familiar, and yet at the same time, so full of ancient power. "I should be scared of you, James Hastin," she said. "Of what you can do."

His eyes flared white for a moment, and he shrugged. "I'm just a djinn. Doing what needed to be done."

"To protect me?"

"That. And to protect the world."

"The world?"

Another flare of white light filled his eyes, and he let out a slow breath. "Syrin was a powerful sorcerer. Powerful enough to be reincarnated when his very existence had been unmade." He brushed his thumb over her cheek again, a gentle swipe of tears she hadn't realized were there. "That kind of power corrupts. The mind, the soul. And with Syrin's memories burning in Philips's head, the world wasn't safe. What he's already done is bad enough. What he would do with Syrin's lust for dominance..." He shook his head.

"So you just saved the world?"

"Yeah." His lips curled in a grin. *His* grin—the sheepish one she loved so much. Had always loved, even when she was Rose and he was Barqan. "But don't tell anyone."

A hot lump filled her throat and she shook her head. "I don't... I don't know what to do with all this."

He lowered his head, nudging his forehead against hers with a soft touch, his eyes closing. "You'll sort it out. You're my Hope," he murmured. "That's what you do."

His Hope. As she'd always been.

Heart joining the lump in her throat, she tilted her head and captured his lips with hers again. Real. He was real. He was hers. And she was his.

A low groan reverberated in his chest, and he pulled away again, framing her face in hands that shook.

Tahlee swallowed, every fiber in her body suddenly prickling with bleak realization.

He was going once more. Leaving her. Her soul told her.

Her heart told her.

"Don't you even think of walking out on me again," she whispered. "Don't you dare."

Opening his eyes, he met her gaze. "You were never

meant to be in danger, Hope. Ever. But knowing me...even *not* knowing me...it's put your life, your very existence at risk. What happened—with Philips and you overhearing him, and Guarded Souls being the agency contacted to protect you—it's too big a coincidence. The Universe... Fate...it has a farking bizarre sense of humor, and us crossing paths like this... Too big a coincidence. If you have anything to do with me...it's too dangerous."

"I don't care." She shook her head, tangling her hand in the hair at his nape. "I'm a flipping investigative journalist in London. My life is at risk every time an article is published with my name in the byline."

He chuckled, the sound wry and sad. It scraped at her. Hollowed her out. "Your life has always been better without knowing me. Look what happened when you were Rose. When I came into your life, when *Barqan* came into it—"

"No!" The word burst from her in a fierce growl. "Do you know what Syrin used to do to me? I remember. Rose's memories, they're here." She tapped her temple. "I remember the abuse, the oppression...the obsession."

"You remember them *now*," he said. "Because of me."

"So? Your point being? I don't care about them. I don't care about who I was before. I care about *now*. About you. I flipping *love* you, James."

His gaze held hers as he touched her cheek again. "Hope—"

Her chest tightened. "Don't," she growled. "Whatever it is you think you're going to do, whatever you think you're going to say, just don't."

Jaw bunching, his Adam's apple jerked in his throat. "I want you to wish you'd never met me at the pub, Hope. A simple wish. Just one. I *need* you to wish for that."

She blinked. "What?"

"I need you to wish you'd never bumped into me at the pub in Piccadilly."

A clammy chill crawled over her skin. She blinked again. "Why? *Why* would you ask me to do that?"

"I can't..." Grief etched his face before he scrubbed at it with a savage hand. "I can't be with you, Tahlee, without loving you. I can't. And loving you means my djinn's heart becomes mortal. If I'm mortal...I can't protect you. I can't keep you safe. Hell, I might die. Dying doesn't scare me, but you, being under any kind of threat...that frightens the shite out of me. So it's better if you'd never met me at the pub. Better we never talked, laughed together, kissed..." His voice broke. "It'll be easier for me to keep you safe and happy if you don't know me. If you live your life without me, if you fall in love with someone else, live out your days with them, not me..."

The cold crept into her heart. Her eyes burned, the backs of them stinging. With tears? Or anger? "I don't want you to keep me safe. I just want *you*, James Hastin. All I want, all I *wish* for, is a life with *you*."

"Hope..." He shook his head. "Think about what happened here today. Think about what *would* have happened if I no longer had my djinn powers."

"I fell in love with *you*, not your power! I couldn't give a rats arse about your power."

His chest swelled with a shaky breath. His eyes searched hers.

"Don't you get it, Hastin?" Emotions warred inside her —sorrow, anger, determination, hope. She let a smile pull at her lips, even as her throat thickened.

"No life I could possibly live without you in it is worth even half the life I would live *with* you. I love you.

I will always love you. No matter who I am, no matter what life I'm living. In this one, or the next, or the next. If I'm not with you, if you're not with me, I will feel it, deep in my very existence. I will know that the life I'm living is wrong. I will know the life I'm living is incomplete. And I'll go searching for you. Subconsciously, I'll always be looking for you. Because we are *meant* to be together."

He stared at her.

She shrugged sadly. "Say you don't feel the same, and I'll shut up. I'll make your damn wish. But if you lie to me, I'll know." Then she stabbed her finger into his chest, turning her stare into a glare. "And of every living soul I've ever met in my life, *you* are the one person, the *only* person, I one-hundred percent trust."

A strangled groan rumbled deep in his chest before he shook his head with a wry smile. "I knew I should have been more duplicitous when we were together."

She chuckled, even as her heart thumped faster. "Yeah, yeah."

He held her gaze.

She arched her eyebrow. "Do you hear what I'm saying, James Hastin? Do you hear me, *Barqan*? I love you. And I know you love me. It'll be okay. I prom—"

"I love you, Tahlee Hope."

She blinked.

Blinked again. Frowned...and blinked a third time.

"Did you...? Holy crap, you said it! Did you just..." She pressed her hand to her mouth, stared at him, and then dropped her hand again. "You just said you love me, right?"

That sheepish grin returned. "Who am I to fight something this real? This true? Since the very moment I saw you, over fourteen hundred years ago, I was a goner. From the second you looked at me, smiled at me, I was yours.

"But I warn you, you'd better be ready for a life with me, because at the first *sign* of a gray hair in my head, I'm going to freak the fark out and probably buy every box of hair dye in Walgreens I can get my hands— Oh. *Buy.* Wow, that's going to take some getting used to. Buying stuff. Wonder if Kade will still keep me on at Guarded Souls? Or I could go back to dog grooming in London if you—"

"Wait." She grabbed at the front of his shirt. "Say it again."

"What?" His lips twitched. "All of what I just said?"

"You know what I mean." She scowled at him. Tugged him a little closer to her. "Say it again. Say 'I love you, Tahlee Hope.' Again."

He laughed. "I love you, Tahlee Hope. Again. I love—"

She yanked him forward by the shirt and kissed him.

And then yanked his shirt up over his head, crawled onto his lap and kissed him some more.

He laughed into her mouth, his hands going to the buttons at the front of her shirt.

She helped him, popping the top one even as she deepened their kiss.

Sure, they were still in the room in which Philips had been dragged to Hell. Sure, they really should find somewhere else. Sure, they had the rest of their lives to kiss in far more appropriate places. And yeah, sure, they probably *should* let Kitt know they were both okay. The last he'd seen of her, she'd been ranting about James being taken by Syrin.

But doing all that meant they'd have to tear their lips from each other's, and no way was she ready to stop kissing James. Not yet.

In ten minutes maybe. Or an hour. Or—

"Err, am I interrupting something?"

Tahlee jerked backward, a squeal bursting out of her as James hauled her closer to his body.

A petite woman wearing cut-off denim shorts, an AC/DC T-shirt, and knee-high Doc Martens smirked at them from a few feet away.

"Shite, Nim," James growled, his arms loosening a little around Tahlee's body. "Knock next time."

Nim? Tahlee studied the new arrival's brilliant blue eyes, bright purple buzzcut, multiple earrings in her right ear, and a constellation tattoo rising up the side of her swanlike neck.

James had mentioned Nim before. Something about her being unable to locate the sorcerer using dark magic. Was she employed by Guarded Souls as well? Was she some kind of paranormal being? Was anyone at the security firm human?

Does it matter?

Nim grinned, flicked a look at Tahlee, and wriggled her beautifully shaped eyebrows at James. "Well, given I came running into the room, ready to thrash it out—*mano a mano*, magic style—with a dark sorcerer, with the sole purpose of saving the very existence of my good djinn friend and his human squeeze, only to find my good djinn friend and his human squeeze making out like a couple of teenagers...I'm going to forgive you for not saying thank you for getting here so quickly and just point out that I kinda *did* knock."

She threw a quick glance over her shoulder toward the door, which now hung on one hinge, the doorknob missing, the place where it used to be a mess of splintered wood.

James snorted. "Well, now you know how into it Hope and I get when we're making out."

Tahlee blinked at the door. How had they not heard that happen?

Turning back to James, she frowned. "We should have heard that."

"I concealed the sound with magic to maintain the element of surprise," Nim said. "However, you should have at least seen the door swinging in." She dropped a wink at Tahlee, blue eyes twinkling. "So, what the hell's going on? Kitt calls me in a frenzy, damn near growling down the phone about you then Ms. Hope here, being taken by the sorcerer. I managed to work out he was saying Doug Philips was an ancient sorcerer called Syrin, who was the sorcerer who originally summoned you a millennia ago, before his anger got the better of him—I think—and he totally wolfed out. Haven't heard from him since, but he's probably sprinting down the Topanga Canyon mountains as we speak, in full wolf form, ready to rip open this Philips's throat."

She looked around the room. "But I don't see a dark sorcerer here. Or even a muted mage, for that matter. So... what's going on, djinn? Talk to me."

Tahlee turned back to James. That thick, hot lump returned to her throat.

Djinn. What were James's work colleagues, his friends, going to say when they discovered what's happened to him? When they learned what he'd done? For *her*?

Would they hate her? Hate *him*? Turn their back on him?

People sucked. She knew that. But did paranormal beings have the same hang-ups about unexpected change?

Her stomach clenched. A prickling heat crawled over

her. God, James had given up everything for her. *Everything*. What if she wasn't worth it? What if—

"Hope and I were snogging over the fact we're going to need to go old-age retirement home shopping together," James said.

Nim blanched. "What?"

He smiled, feathered a thumb over Tahlee's cheek, and then grinned up at Nim. "Amongst all the mayhem of fighting *and* defeating, Syrin—BTW, he's been dragged to Hell. Literally. So sorry, but no epic magic battle for you, young lady—I accepted the fact I love this amazing, incredible, fierce, brave, sexy woman here," he smiled at Tahlee again. "And in so doing, surrendered my djinn's heart."

Nim's eyebrows shot up. "You *what*?"

He chuckled, smoothing his hands up and down Tahlee's back. "I'm mortal. I think. Don't know if I'm human, as such, but I'm no longer a djinn. So next time you want a Cinnabon, Nim, you're going to have to buy one. Tahlee and I, meanwhile, are going to be planning for our long life of playing Bridge together, drinking tea, and complaining about the youth of today." He frowned. "That's what old people do, right?"

Stomach still clenching, chest tight, Tahlee let out a shaky breath. "I wish I had a cup of tea right—"

An exquisite bone china cup and saucer set appeared in her hand. The very Tiffany teacup and saucer set she'd seen online and drooled over one morning while in bed with James a month into living together. The one with the delicate gray leaf pattern and fine silver trim.

She stared at it, the distinct aroma of Earl Grey with a hint of lemon teasing and tantalizing her senses. "Wh-what?"

Lifting her stare to James, the tea cup wobbling on the saucer as her hand trembled, she frowned. "Wh... *How*? Did you do that?"

He gaped at the tea in her hand. Frowned. Squinted at the cup some more and rubbed at the back of his head. "I did. The second you said 'I wish I had a cup of tea,' I remembered this teacup and saucer you went crazy over and, well...there it is." Shaking his head, he touched the cup with a finger, as if it could at any moment bite him. "And I felt the rush. In fact, it's still rushing through me. But I don't..." With another shake of his head, he looked up at her. "I don't understand."

"Wait wait wait," Nim muttered, crouching down beside them. She lifted her hands toward his head, giving Tahlee an apologetic smile. "Can I just...?"

Heart racing, Tahlee scrambled off James's lap, placed the tea cup and saucer on the floor, and inched away from it.

Everything felt cold. He was *still* a djinn. His heart...

She swallowed, watching Nim place her fingers on his temples. If he was still a djinn, if he still had his djinn's heart, did that mean, despite what he said, he didn't truly love her?

Oh God. Could that be the case?

Pulse pounding, she crawled away a few feet.

"Hope?" Confusion filled his voice. She looked at him. Bewilderment swam in his green eyes. "This isn't what you're thinking," he said.

She didn't know *what* she was thinking.

"Tell me," Nim said, a steely tone in the command, "exactly—no paraphrasing—exactly what curse Syrin cast on you with his dying breath fourteen hundred years ago."

James jerked his stare back to Nim. "How did you know?"

"Kitt told me everything, Jimmy Boy. The wolf shifter's been worried about you." Nim walked her fingertips over his temples, the digits moving in a spider-like dance that made Tahlee's pulse quicken. "Now tell me, word for word, what Syrin said. I need to hear the curse as he uttered it."

Eyes wide, chest heaving, James stared at her. "*Quod si te iterum vocem suam verbum potestate cor tuum non morieris.*"

A hot finger traced up Tahlee's spine at the words. Latin? Maybe?

Nim's frown deepened. "If you love again and utter its word, your heart's power will die. That was the curse?"

"That was it. He said a miscreant like me didn't deserve love. He said I didn't..." He gave Tahlee a glance. "I didn't deserve Rose, and was pretty farking adamant he'd use his dying breath to make sure I would never love again. And then he cast the curse: *Quod si te iterum vocem suam verbum potestate cor tuum non morieris.*"

Eyes narrow, Nim studied him.

And snorted out a low laugh.

Tahlee blinked.

James frowned. "Are you laughing at me, wiccan?"

Lips tight, Nim shook her head—and then burst out laughing, hands dropping from his head to slap at her thighs. "You idiot, Hastin!"

"Hey hey hey," he pouted. "Words hurt, Nim. Words hurt."

"Exactly." She slapped at his shoulder with the back of her hand, twisted around to grin at Tahlee, and then turned back to James, slapping his shoulder again. "You of all people should be aware of the power of words, Jimmy

Boy. The *right* words. Sure, Syrin's curse was a nasty one, a mean one. But it was clumsy wording, which meant it had a flaw. It needed one crucial element to work. An element you never gave it."

"I never..." James frowned. "What the farking hell are you going on about, Nim. Is this a witch thing?"

She laughed louder, throwing Tahlee another smile. "Don't you get it? The curse required you to fall in love again. *Again*! How can you fall in love *again* when you've never stopped loving Rose in the first place?"

She looked at Tahlee once more. "With you. He's been in love with you forever. He never *stopped* being in love with you. In case you missed the point I was trying to—"

"I got it," Tahlee chuckled through a tight throat. She looked at James, staring at her, spine straight, green eyes wide. "I get it. I remember the night he promised me—Rose, I mean—that he would love me forever. I remember those words whispered into my ear as if he only whispered them yesterday." She smiled, holding his stare. "And it turns out he really meant them."

His nostrils flared.

She let out a soft laugh. "See? There's a reason you're the only person I've truly trusted in my entire life, Hastin. It's because you've never lied to me. You kept your promise for over a thousand years."

His nostrils flared again, and then—in a blur of purple smoke—he stood directly in front of her. "Hey, Hope?" Hand extended to her, he gave her another sheepish grin. "Any chance you want to spend the rest of your life with a djinn?"

Heart racing, she slipped her fingers around his and let him help her to her feet. "I told you. The only life I want is a life with you, James. Djinn or not. And you know me. I'm a stickler for telling the truth."

His eyes flared white for a second, and then he cupped her face in his hands and nudged his forehead to hers. "It's never going to be boring, but it might be a little dangerous at times."

"Bring it on," she whispered.

He chuckled.

"And on that note," Nim muttered, "I'm out of here. Going to fill in Kade on what's going on and see if I can track down Kitt. The poor guy's paws are probably killing him by now."

James lifted his head. "Want me to...y'know," he splayed his fingers with a quick flick, "*poof* you to him?"

Nim shook her head. "I've got my own means. My broom is outside." She grinned at Tahlee. "Kidding."

She headed for the door. Tahlee watched her for a second, and then buried her fingers into James's hair and pulled his head down to hers. "I wish for a kiss," she growled.

"Granted," he whispered, a second before crushing her lips with his.

"By the way?" Nim's raised voice reached them from the door and, with an impatient groan, James dragged his lips from Tahlee's.

"Why haven't you gone yet?" he asked, smoothing his hands around Tahlee's back to draw her closer. "I've got a wish to grant."

Nim studied him for a second, lips curling, and waved a finger toward Tahlee. "Did either of you know Ms. Hope there is a sorcerer?"

Tahlee blinked. "A what?"

"A what?" James echoed.

A dimple flashed in Nim's check. "Or sorceress, if you don't want to be PC. A damn powerful one, what with the vibes I'm picking up from her. I guess it's in her blood. Pretty certain that means she's going to live for a long freaking time, yes? Hope you two pick a good old-people's home."

And with a jaunty little wave, she walked through the door, leaving them alone in the room.

"Did she just say..." Tahlee began.

James smiled, mischief dancing on his face. "We are going to have so much farking fun, my sorceress," he declared. "Fancy a fuck on the beach in Fiji?"

She rolled her hips and squeezed his arse. "I *wish* for a fuck on a beach in Fiji, my djinn," she said.

Eyes glowing white, smile turning to a wicked grin, James raised his hand beside his face. "Done," he murmured.

And clicked his fingers.

EPILOGUE

Andy Gribble stopped on the sidewalk and, tilting his head back, read the sign above the closed door—The Tarnished Spur—before swiping at his mouth.

He lowered his gaze from the sign and looked at the red-painted wooden double door.

His life had changed so much since the last time he'd hurried through it.

Who would have thought it was only forty-eight hours since he'd drifted into the bar, dejected, miserable, ready to drink himself into oblivion? It felt like forever.

So much had changed since that morning.

Morning. Ha. Looking to get good and drunk at eight am. Shoot, he'd been a pathetic idiot, ready to drown his sorrows in cheap beer, willing to throw everything away…

Except he hadn't. Thanks to a conversation with a stranger whose name he'd never gotten.

No, no…he *had* gotten the man's name. James. James something. But his friends called him…

"Jimmy," he murmured, with a smile.

If it hadn't been for his conversation with Jimmy, who knows what he would have done that morning. What Betsy would have done.

Throat thick, he studied the door again. If he walked into the bar right now, would he find Jimmy there?

He hoped not. It wasn't the best of places. There was a reason he'd ended up there himself that morning. But still, it'd be nice to say thank you to the man.

Grunting out a laugh, he shook his head at the closed door. "Wish I could tell you how much you helped me that morning, Jimmy. Wherever you—"

"Andy?"

Andy startled, swinging around at the sound of the familiar voice.

Jimmy stood on the sidewalk, dressed in faded blue jeans and a T-shirt with the image of a bear in a hat, from that old '70s puppet show. A wide smile stretched his lips, and he extended his hand toward Andy. "It *is* you! I thought it was. Small world, 'eh?"

A smile spreading over his own face, Andy snagged Jimmy's hand and gave it an enthusiastic pump. "I was just thinking about you," he said, unable to keep the delight from his voice. "Wishing I could bump into you again."

"Oh yeah?" Jimmy raised his eyebrows, an infectious happiness in his expression. "And why's that?"

"I did what you told me to do," Andy said. He tried not to puff out his chest, but he couldn't help himself. "Remember? In there? When I was miserable because I'd had a fight with Betsy? You told me to be courageous and tell her how I felt about her. I went back home straight from this place, straight after our conversation, and told her how much I loved her. Told her that I breathe for her. Begged her forgiveness for being a jackass."

"Hey, well done." Jimmy nudged his shoulder with a gentle fist. "Knew you had it in you."

"You helped me. So much."

Jimmy pressed his hand to his chest and dipped into a playful half bow. "I'm glad I could. You're a good man, Andy Gribble. Can I assume Betsy forgave you?"

"She did." A wave of warmth flowed through Andy. His face ached from smiling so much. "In fact, we're renewing our vows next weekend. Putting on a fancy shindig and everything." He pointed at Jimmy, eyes widening. "Hey, you need to come. If it wasn't for…"

He trailed off when Jimmy shook his head, his disappointment tempered by the friendly smile on the other man's face.

"I'd love to come, dude," Jimmy said, sliding his hands into his back pockets. "I really would. But I'll be swapping my *own* vows that day."

"You'll be…" Andy smacked at his thigh. "Oh wow, you're getting married?"

Jimmy smiled. "I am. To the woman I've loved since the second I saw her."

Andy beamed. "That's beautiful. Wonderful! Can't wish for anything better than that, can you."

"Nope, my friend." Jimmy smiled, and for a second, it was as if the sun turned his eyes white. "You truly can't."

EPILOGUE II

Cold.

Dark. And cold.

Everything was dark and cold.

Opening his eyes, Kitt struggled to sit up.

Pain sheared through him, from his side right all the way to his left shoulder.

He winced, pressing a hand to his rib, and hissed at the fresh wave of pain lashing through him.

What the...

The last thing he remembered was running through a tract of dense trees in wolf form, heading for the LA base of Douglas Philips.

The bastard had taken James. Had summoned him somehow. And then he'd taken Tahlee Hope ,as well.

Nim had found James's location, called Kitt and told him it was okay, she was going to help. But that wasn't enough.

Kitt had to get there. James needed help.

He'd shifted into his wolf form and started running.

And then...here.

But how?

Straightening a little—biting back another surge of pain at the minuscule movement—he squinted into the darkness.

Tiny shards of faint light glinted off something a few feet away from him.

He frowned and, grinding his teeth against the agony he knew would come, climbed to his feet and crossed the darkness.

Bars.

Gut knotting, he reached out and grabbed one of them.

"Shit!" he yelped, staggering back a step as excruciating anguish lanced through his palm and up his arm.

Silver. The bars were made of silver.

"What the..." he muttered, turning slowly. Where *was* he? And how did he get here?

"Hello?" he called, wincing as the unseen wound in his side protested.

His shout bounced around him, fading into nothing.

Silence hung heavy again, oppressive and thick and cold.

Kitt swallowed, the hairs at the back of his neck standing on end. What the hell was going—

"Ah, you're finally conscious," a deep, disembodied voice wafted to him from the darkness. "Excellent. That makes me very happy. I knew I'd one day catch the last dire wolf in existence...and I'd hate to think I'd mortally wounded you when I had."

THANK YOU

If you enjoyed **Hope's Wish**, follow Lexxie on Bookbub for pre-order, sales and new-release alerts. Sign-up for her newsletter, the Lexxicon to receive a free copy of her (erotic) paranormal short story, **The Cavern**, plus never miss out on exciting announcements and giveaways!

ABOUT LEXXIE COUPER

Lexxie writes fun-with-feels romances. She lives with a manic rescue dog, a self-absorbed rescue cat, a very patient husband not rescued from anything, and two strong-willed teenage daughters who will one day rule the world.

Lexxie lives by two simple rules – measure your success not by how much money you have, but by how often you laugh, and always try everything at least once. As a consequence, she's laughed her way through many an eyebrow raising adventure. You can find details of her writing at
www.LexxieCouper.com

Amber's
HEAT

Guarded Souls Book Three

LEXXIE COUPER

AMBER'S HEAT

GUARDED SOULS, BOOK THREE

Available Now in Print and Digital

Who is the hunted, and the hunter?

He's been a lone wolf for centuries, the last of his species. A secret. And then she enters his life. But is she the future he'd never imagined he could have...or is she his worst nightmare?

Kitt Newton accepted the fact he's the last known dire wolf shifter on the planet centuries ago. He's okay with that. Work keeps him busy. Can't think about being alone when he's busy protecting people—humans—after all. And who really needs to be mated for life? However, when he's captured by a mysterious hunter, the last person he expects to save him is Amber Calegari, a woman he met at a café a few weeks ago.

Amber has spent her life studying dinosaurs. Specifically *canis dirus* from the late Pleistocene period. She'd thought she'd gone mad when she found evidence of an ancient human/dire wolf species. And even madder when she followed the trail to LA...and a man called Kitt Newton. Surely the massive hunk of burly hotness couldn't be some kind of paranormal creature? Right? And if he is, shouldn't she—as a scientist—reveal his existence to the world?

An apex predator has no right being draw to a weak, fragile human, but is Kitt mistaken about Amber? And if he is, what the hell is he going to do about it, especially when the hunter is closing in again...

ALSO BY LEXXIE COUPER

Fire Mates Series

Sera's Dragon
How to Love Your Dragon
Crouching Tigress, Sexy Dragon
Enter The Dragon
Dragon, Interrupted

Guarded Souls Series

Destiny's Knight
Hope's Wish
Amber's Heat

Dark Sentinel Series

Dark Destiny
Dark Embrace

Savage Australis Series

Savage Retribution
Savage Transformation